Little Gems

Sunstone

ROMANCE WRITERS *of Australia*

Little Gems

**Anthology of Short Stories published by
Romance Writers of Australia Inc
© 2016**

ISBN 978-0-9872809-4-7

**Little Gems Coordinator: Lis Hoorweg
Order Manager: Shannon Curtis
Editor: Joan Wright
Digital Formatting: Lana Pecherczyk
Cover Design: Sheridan Kent**

Little Gems

Sunstone

Short Story Anthology
2016

ROMANCE WRITERS
of Australia

Autographs

Contributing Authors

Foreword

Leisl Leighton

Stories

Solar Flare

The Sunstone Heart

The Heart of Stone

Follow Your Dreams

Breaking Free

In the Cards

An Enticing Proposition

Say the Words

The Sunstone Bride

The Sunstone Inheritance

Lights Will Guide You Home

Treasure and Trust

The Healing Gift

For the Love of a Pug

Cover Art

Sheridan Kent

Contents

Foreword

The modern sunstone, called such because of the golden/yellow colour emitted by the red copper flakes embedded in its crystals, is rare. It is only found in the United States, Norway and Siberia—vastly different places that share the same core ingredients needed to make this unique and pretty stone.

The old sunstone seems to be a completely different crystal altogether. Thought to be cordierite or Iceland spar—a stone that looks like ice—it appears in medieval Icelandic texts where it's used as an allegory for the Virgin, who, like the sunstone, allowed a ray of sunlight through to the world. It also appears in Icelandic mythology as a stone the Vikings used to navigate their way at sea. It was purported that by holding it up, a person could find the sun in a cloudy sky or on a snowy day.

A thoroughly useful tool, but also a beautiful and romantic one.

It seems to me that the sunstone could also be the birthstone of all romance writers. Like a sunstone, a romance writer glows from within for the stories they must tell, and the characters for whom they must find a *Happily Ever After* or *Happily For Now*. Like a sunstone, reading romance is the comfort read for those who are troubled, a ray of sunshine breaking through on a cloudy day. We, as romance writers, feel this, too, as that ray breaks through when we sit down to write or read the treasured words of others. And like the sunstone, we are each unique and rare, with our own stories to tell, our own joy to share with the world. No matter our vastly different origins or backgrounds, we share the same core ingredients needed to become a writer.

It gives me great pleasure to introduce these *Sunstone Little Gems* stories with you this year, stories that share the core ingredient of joy in people finding love despite all the obstacles. I know you will feel warmed by the sunstones in these stories as you read the treasure of words and romance within.

And finally, I hope all of you will always have a sunstone in your life to guide your way even in the darkest of times.

Leisl Leighton
President
Romance Writers of Australia

Solar Flare

By

Suzanne Cass

Tipping her head back, Lissa let the sunlight flow over her. Not caring that the touch of the sun's rays would add to the smattering of freckles already adorning her features, she delighted in the warmth stroking her cheeks. Opening her eyes, she took in the simple endless blue above.

How she loved the sun. It'd taken some getting used to, the merciless sunshine that hounded her all day. But now, after seven weeks, she was becoming familiar with the terrible heat of the West Australian outback.

The animal beneath her writhed, bringing her awareness back to the dusty yard.

'Lissa, watch what you're doin'!'

She gave an involuntary start at Barry's loud reprimand.

'Sorry, boss.' Blowing a lock of flaming auburn hair out of her eyes, she tightened her grip on the calf's front leg, leaning all the weight into her right knee to hold down its bony head. The calf rolled the whites of its eyes, naïve and terrified. It let out a muffled bellow, raising a plume of dust from the ground with its breath. Lissa agreed with the

9

sentiment behind the calf's cry. Branding was a disturbing, painful experience.

'Orright, let 'im go.'

Lissa leapt up, watching the calf scramble for a footing, raising a choking red cloud as it found its feet and took off towards the cattle yard fence.

'Only a few more to go, hey?' Barry let out a loud, belly-shaking whoop. Lissa raised a tight smile.

'Aww, come on kid, it ain't that bad.' He gave a sly waggle of one of his bushy eyebrows and she had to smile back. Barry had taken a little getting used to as well, but now she found the leading station hand was growing on her too. 'Well, go and grab another one then,' he said, turning his back to ready the branding iron for the next calf.

'I'll give you a hand, if you like.'

Lissa whipped her head around at the unexpected closeness of the deep, masculine voice. Ace. His dimple-wreathed grin made her forget for a second exactly where she was. Lost for words, she stared up at him. God he was tall. Even taller than her, and not many men could say that. Watching her from beneath the brim of his hat, he eventually raised an arm and pointed towards the bawling bundle of calves in the adjoining yard.

'You know, with the calves.'

'Sure,' she stammered. Following him towards the holding yard, she watched his long jean-clad legs stride out, his faded cowboy boots scuffing through the dust. Ace was the station owner's youngest son. The very gorgeous youngest son. Of course she'd noticed him. She'd noticed him the very first day she'd taken the job on this isolated cattle station. But she was just one of the many hired hands to drift through the peripheries of his life. She could count the number of times she'd spoken to him on one hand. Now here he was, offering her his help.

Ace chose their next victim and together they dragged the bucking tangle of brown hide into the middle of the yard and wrangled it to the ground in front of Barry. Lissa knelt in the dirt next to Ace, close, almost touching him. She could feel his proximity through the cotton of her shirt. She inhaled the heady scent of heat and dust; and something else. Him. It was him she could smell, a mixture of sweat and sunbeams and musky leather.

'How long you been out here now?' He was trying to make conversation. Her mouth felt dry. Talking to guys was not one of her strong points, especially not good-looking ones who stared at her with an air of expectancy.

'It'll be two months on Friday.' She brushed several of the ever present flies away from her face.

'Worked up north before?'

She shook her head.

'You don't say much do you?' He shot another of his winning grins in her direction. 'You're different from the rest.'

She opened her mouth to tell him it wasn't true when the calf gave a desperate heave, and her words were lost in a grunt as she struggled to control the animal.

'Nice necklace,' Ace said, once the calf was still again, his gaze dropping to the opening V of her shirt.

'Thanks,' she replied, reaching up to touch it reflexively. 'It's a sunstone pendant.'

'That's a good name for it. It's got all the colours of the sun in there.'

'Yeah … I got it when I was living in Melbourne. They don't get too much sunshine down there,' she added.

He studied Lissa through side-slanted eyes. 'Well, it's nice. It matches your hair.'

What the hell? Was he flirting with her?

Ace brought his gaze up from her pendant and let his eyes rest on her face. *Outstanding eyes.* The abstract thought made her blink in surprise. Where had that come from? Even if he did have glorious rich chocolate eyes that reminded her of her grandmother's fudge brownies, he was off limits. Wasn't he?

One morning, a few days after she arrived, she'd been struggling to saddle one of the horses when Ace had appeared as if from nowhere, offering assistance. But no sooner had he lifted the saddle out of her arms than his father, the station owner, had appeared and commanded Ace come and give him a hand. As they'd walked away, Lissa had overheard his father talking to Ace in a low, stern voice about his responsibilities on the farm, and how they *didn't* include flirting with any of the seasonal stock hands. Ace had argued that it was all just harmless, but his father had stalled him with a dismissive wave of his hand and walked away, leaving Ace glowering at his back.

Yep, he was definitely off limits.

Before she could think of an answer to his intriguing comment, Barry said, 'Orright, let 'im go,' and they set off to drag another calf over.

'You know, you remind me of an old pocket watch I used to have, it always ticked and the hands always went around and around like they should, but it never did show the exact right time.' His fingers brushed over hers as they grappled together for the next frightened calf. His touch left a burning trail over her skin, the tingling heat flowing up her arm and into her body.

'Really? Are you saying I'm broken?' She allowed her teeth to show in a smile, to hide the fact he caused such a reaction in her.

'No, that's not what I meant.' He stumbled over the words. 'You're not broken. Just … unusual. You seem to like your own company.'

'Is there anything wrong with that?'

'No, not at all.'

She could still feel the texture of his hands on her skin.

'I'm not trying to be rude. I'm just not much of a conversationalist,' she said, shrugging her acceptance of her self-proclaimed flaw.

'That's okay, I can talk enough for the both of us,' he replied, wading into the milling throng of brown and tan hides. She took the chance to inspect his tall, lean frame, noticing the muscles of his shoulder flexing beneath the material of his T-shirt. He was the complete package, good-looking, hardworking, with the backing of a rich family. Surely he had a girlfriend? They were probably lining up from all over the district.

Snaffling up a passing calf, he caught it without effort in strong arms. She watched his biceps bulge as the calf kicked half-heartedly and then he straightened, staring at her.

'Why don't we have a drink one night, and I'll prove I can do witty repartee when I want to.' The words spilled from her mouth before she could stop them.

'All right then. I'll come tonight. And I'll bring the beer.' He grappled with the back of the calf, Lissa belatedly grabbing the front legs and helping him carry it over to Barry.

'Sure,' she answered weakly, kneeling on the ground next to the calf. *Shit.* What had she just done?

Kneeling in the dirt, waiting for Barry and the branding iron, Lissa let her gaze drift to the horizon, blurring into distance with an absence of defined borders. If the city had been her cage then the desert was her liberty. Ever since she'd left Melbourne after her father died a year ago, it was as if a terrible weight had lifted from her shoulders. She'd thrown her meagre possessions into the back of her battered yellow ute, and escaped, letting the bitumen take her where it wanted, seeking the sun wherever she went.

The resonant warble of a magpie reawakened her awareness and she dropped her gaze back to the dusty yard. And now the sun had led her here. To this cattle station in the outback. To where Ace crouched beside her, his nearness setting the tiny hairs on her arm standing up to attention. Her heart gave a surprising kick beneath her ribs when she thought about this gorgeous man who wanted to have a beer with her.

~ * ~

Ace tapped on the door to her cabin, the sound reverberating through the evening sky. What the hell was he doing here? He almost turned on his heel and walked away, but then he heard her say, 'Hi Ace.' Sweeping the door open, she let it clang back on its metal hinges. Tonight her curves were softened by a long, flowing skirt that swished across the floor, her fiery hair loose, long strands flying around her round face. Did she know how gorgeous she looked, standing there, hands on hips, framed by the open door?

'Beer,' he said, holding up a sixpack, offering her a genuine smile. He was here, he couldn't back out now.

'Thanks. Shall we go sit round the back?' She was nervous, he could tell by the slight quaver in her voice. Her nerves were echoed in his own churning stomach. But his nerves were more from the thought of what his father would say if he found out he was here. Ace withstood the urge to cast a quick glance over his shoulder.

'Sounds good.' He followed her through the tiny cabin and out the back door. Outside there was an array of mismatched chairs to choose from. The air still held heat from the late afternoon sun's rays and the air chimed with the sounds of frogs calling from the nearby tank stand.

'What's that?' Ace indicated the strange shape, all odd angles and long legs, reminiscent of an intoxicated spider.

'It's a solar telescope. I like to look at the sun.' Was that a defensive hitch he heard in her tone?

He strolled over to the contraption and placed a hand on the smooth metallic surface. 'Can I take a look?'

'Sure, go ahead.' She gestured towards the telescope. 'There're supposed to be some great solar flares erupting today. I've got it trained on a large sunspot—that's the darker spot you can see on the surface,' she said, her hands moving in an enthusiastic dance. It was the most animated he'd ever seen her. As she talked, her cheeks flushed pink as a rose, and he found himself not really listening to the rest of what she was saying, instead fighting the urge to run a finger down the curve of her creamy cheek. Would her skin be as soft as it looked? He'd wanted to find out the answer to that question from the very first day she'd walked into the machinery shed. Even though her clothes had been creased and dishevelled from her five hour drive to reach the isolated homestead and her red hair escaping from her ponytail was all wispy and knotted, he'd noticed her pale beauty. And those sombre grey eyes. Eyes that held mysteries, hidden behind her reserved gaze.

Lissa wasn't a conventional beauty. She was tall, nearly as tall as him, her curves generous, with full round breasts and long legs. Nothing like the slim-hipped, small-breasted women, with easy smiles and self-confident charm he was usually drawn to. His father would give Lissa her marching orders without a second thought if he knew what Ace was doing tonight. Fraternising with the station hands was against his father's rules. She wasn't good enough for his youngest son. Lissa was a drifter, with no true home, no money, no connections, searching for something intangible. An outsider. Ace was expected to marry into outback aristocracy, find a good wife, with good breeding, who understood how things worked in their harsh country.

But in the past few weeks, Ace had found himself instinctively drawn to Lissa's presence, watching for her in the stock yards before they mounted up for a day of mustering, or studying her out of the corner of his eye as she stood, kicking up the ochre dust with the rest of the station hands at smoko, drinking billy tea. Then he would catch a glimpse of her red hair caught in the sun's rays, and it was like a match flaring in the dark recesses of his soul. He'd fought his involuntary inclinations, turning away from her every time she came near. And yet, look where he found himself now. As if his legs had walked themselves over to Lissa's cottage of their own volition.

'Sorry, what did you say?' he apologised, leaning forward and looking through the eyepiece, hoping to hide his discomfit at being caught out not listening. Wow, the vista through the viewfinder was amazing, intense fiery colours assaulted his eyes.

'My dad gave it to me, just before he died.' The statement was quiet, a breath of wind blowing through the evening air.

'Oh.' Ace could feel the weight behind her words. He kept staring though the ocular lens, watching the luminescent orange surface of the sun curve through the plane of his vision, so bright it almost hurt his eyes.

'You miss your dad?' The statement was a foreign one for him. His father was a hard man, shaped by the tough realities of eking out a living from the land, the pressure of constant droughts and dust and cattle prices. The kind of man Ace knew he didn't ever want to become.

'Yeah.' She was silent for long enough that he finally looked up from the telescope to see her standing close to him, her fingers touching the small pendant which rested in the hollow of her throat. 'He gave me this pendant too. He said it would give me courage and independence.'

'Sunstones must be rare. I've never seen one before. It's beautiful.' *Like you.* He had to force the words back down his throat. On impulse he reached up and took the necklace between his fingers, to feel the weight of the alien stone. The dying rays of the sun caught it, making it shimmer and glow, as if from a hidden source of light within. The movement brought him closer to her. He could see a tiny vein in her neck, beating along with the tattoo of her heart. Prickles of sensation ran beneath his skin, a feeling of recognition.

Rearranging his facial muscles into the semblance of a smile he said, 'I reckon these sunstones might be the closest thing to magic I've ever seen.'

'I think so too.' She touched his hand. A fleeting brush of her fingertips over his palm as he played with the sunstone. Then she gave a coaxing laugh. 'That's one of the reasons I wanted to come and work in the outback. Everything in the sky is so bright and alive, as if it's going to jump down the telescope at me.' Her long skirt brushed the ground, making a whispering sound. 'And because of the kind of people I've met out here.' Her eyes narrowed ever so slightly. She wasn't laughing now, the lines on her face smooth, her plump lips parted and fascinating. The hot evening air felt still, the silence clinging like a shroud.

He wanted to kiss her. The urge flowed through him like an unstoppable wave. He closed his eyes against the craving.

'Are you okay?' she asked, her soft voice washing over him. He managed to open his eyes again. They were still standing so close, her pendant still resting in his fingers.

Sure, never been better, he wanted to say, but the words wouldn't come. He wanted to back away from her, dismiss her with a flippant wave of his hand. But he'd underestimated Lissa and the effect she had on him. It was unfair, the ease of how she burrowed her way into his awareness. Into his heart and soul.

'You're a fascinating woman, Lissa.' The five words seemed to form echoes of themselves, rebounding back to his ears over and over again. She grinned, her rosy cheeks alight with surprise. His father was going to hate this.

Ace leaned in and let his lips graze hers.

'Oh …' she whispered, her mouth moving beneath his. But she didn't back away. In fact she did the opposite. Her hand snaked up to rest at the nape of his neck, gently, inexorably pulling him in, letting the pressure of her lips increase until he was kissing her long, and deep and slow. Lissa was so warm and welcoming and alive, and he wanted her more than any other woman before. He was baffled by the change that was taking place inside him—in his heart. And in that moment he knew he would do anything, go anywhere, give up everything to be with her.

The Sunstone Heart

By

Heidi Catherine

The woman seated across the table from Cara was disappointingly ordinary. Where were her long, black fingernails? The scarf draped mysteriously over her head? The pagan symbol dangling from her neck? She didn't even have a crystal ball.

Her name was Mary and she looked just like any other ordinary Mary you might run into at the supermarket. She wasn't what Cara had expected a real, live clairvoyant to look like. She didn't look that different to Cara herself. They could probably pass as sisters with their long brown hair and slim build.

Even Mary's clothing was ordinary. Cara looked more closely at her black pants and green cotton shirt, certain she had the exact same items in her own wardrobe. Weren't psychics supposed to wear kaftans or something?

Mary had been highly recommended by Cara's friend, Stella, who said she was spookily accurate. She *knew* things. It was like she had a third eye that could see directly into the centre of your heart and read all the secrets you hid there. She could even read the secrets you didn't know you had.

Stella had spoken at length about her session with Mary while Cara listened with the ears of the sceptic and the heart of a believer. She wanted to believe, but couldn't dislodge the filter that sat behind her ears.

Mary hadn't known Stella's secrets. She'd picked up on clues Stella hadn't even realised she'd dropped.

Still, it was worth a shot. She could no longer deny something was missing from her life. Or rather, *someone.* Specifically someone named Flynn.

Mary shuffled her tarot cards, placed them on the table and tapped them.

'Split the deck twice to make three piles,' she instructed.

Cara did as she was told, wondering if Mary had noticed her grandmother's ring, which she'd worn as a decoy. There was a time she'd worn a real wedding ring, but that seemed long ago. There was nothing more effective at erasing happy memories than a messy divorce. She felt like the only woman in history whose husband had left her for an *older* woman.

Mary lay out nine cards in the shape of a cross, then fixed her gaze on Cara, causing her to shift in her seat as she tried to shake the feeling that this ordinary woman really was seeing the secrets in her heart.

'You have a sadness about you, like you feel something is missing,' said Mary.

How had she known that? She'd done her best to smile when she walked in. That'd been easy. It was a mask she was used to wearing. It fooled her students when they slid into their seats in her English classes at the private girls' school she taught at. It seemed Mary wasn't so easily fooled.

'We're all missing something, aren't we?' said Cara, keeping her answer vague.

'I see you in a profession where you give a lot of yourself. Nursing or teaching?'

Not so hard to guess. There must be thousands of female teachers and nurses.

Cara nodded, deciding it was safe to share this detail. 'I'm a teacher.'

'You do more than that, though, don't you? I see you helping people on a deeper level, far away from home.'

She pinched her lips into a smile. 'That's right.'

She'd spent her last summer holiday in Sri Lanka as a volunteer at an orphanage. Watching a child's face light up as she read them a book was so much more satisfying than handing out copies of *Pride and Prejudice* to a group of girls who'd go home and toss it aside with one hand as they downloaded the movie with the other.

'Is there an area of your life you'd like me to focus on?' Mary's brows furrowed.

'Just tell me whatever it is you think I need to hear.'

She wasn't going to fall for that trap. This was a well-known fishing tactic. Mary was going to need to work for her seventy-five bucks.

'Do you have a piece of jewellery I could hold? Your ring perhaps?'

So she had noticed it.

Seeing no harm, she handed it over and Mary closed it in the palm of her hand.

'This ring belonged to someone else, didn't it?'

Cara nodded. Antique rings generally had been owned by someone else.

'Your grandmother?'

'Yes.' Another lucky guess.

'Your grandmother wants you to know that she loves you.'

'She died before I was born. She never met me.'

She smiled at having tripped Mary up at last. Her grandmother had never had the chance to love her.

'That doesn't prevent her from loving you. She's here now,' said Mary.

Cara glanced around the room, then scolded herself. What did she expect to see? A hologram of her grandmother floating in a corner? Curtains billowing as a cold wind swept through the closed window?

'What does Grandma have to say?' she asked.

'She wants you to wear her ring more often.'

Cara felt a flush race to her cheeks. Not only did Mary know this wasn't an engagement ring, but she also knew she rarely wore it.

'She's concerned you spend so much time worrying about the happiness of others that you forget to nurture the person whose happiness is of the highest importance.'

'Who?' She was certain she hadn't forgotten anybody. She was a dutiful daughter, supportive sister and doting aunt. She looked after her students and always let her friends know how much they meant to her.

'You, of course,' laughed Mary. 'Do you know what stone this is?'

She shook her head. It was a reddish, brown colour, dull from years of sitting in the bottom of her jewellery box.

'It's a sunstone,' said Mary. 'Sunstone reminds us that if we wish to help others, then first we need to be kind to ourselves. It's time for Cara to start looking after Cara.'

She let out a long sigh as she fought back tears. She shouldn't let Mary's words affect her, yet she knew what she said was true. She was burning out, not sleeping, skipping meals and crying when she watched the evening news. There was so much sadness in the world. She tried her best to make a difference, but there was only so much one person could do.

Mary handed the ring back.

'Slip it on your necklace. When worn as a pendant, sunstone brings the wisdom of your heart into alignment with your thoughts.'

Cara threaded the ring onto her chain. It wouldn't harm to at least give it a try. Going into this reading, she'd been acutely aware of the fracture between what her heart wanted to believe and what her mind was allowing it to. And here she was being given a way to bridge that divide.

'You have happiness ahead,' said Mary. 'I can feel it. A great love is about to come your way.'

'I gave up on love years ago,' Cara said a little too quickly, unsure if she was trying to convince Mary or herself.

There was no sense in trying to convince herself that she didn't want Flynn. She'd wanted him since the moment his deep, blue eyes had locked on her own as she swept up the yard at the orphanage. He was tall and wiry and looked about thirty, not much older than her. He wasn't what you'd call traditionally good-looking, but he had a spark about him. The sort that told her he was kind and funny and sweet. It was a spark that made him the most handsome man she'd ever seen.

She had such a physical response to him, she'd almost dropped her broom. Her palms were sweating, her legs were shaking and her heart was beating louder than the squeals of the children who played around her feet.

Then the filter in her brain shut down her thoughts. Getting involved with Flynn would only lead to heartbreak. Plus she didn't have time. Her parents needed her help more often these days. And the demands of her job were intense. She wasn't sure how she ever managed to fit a relationship into her life, let alone a whole marriage.

So she'd kept Flynn at a friendly distance, accepting his invitation on Facebook, but not his invitation to dinner.

'Try talking with your heart,' said Mary. 'Have you really given up?'

She shrugged. 'Maybe not completely.'

Was the sunstone working its magic on her already? She'd told herself that love was beyond her reach as a way of protecting her heart. But did her heart need protection? If she let the guard fall would she really be in that much danger?

'Is there anything else you'd like to ask me about?' Mary turned and glanced at the clock on the wall.

'I think I've heard what I needed.' She stood and brushed an imaginary crease from her pants. 'Say 'bye to Grandma for me.'

Mary laughed. 'You can never say goodbye to Grandma. She's with you always.'

'Sounds like a trailer for a horror movie.'

'Or it could be the beginning of a great love story. Let's wait and see.'

~ * ~

'Tell me everything. Start at the beginning. Go!'

Stella's eyes were wide, curiosity burning behind her long lashes. She pushed a dark curl behind her ear, crossed her arms over her full bosom and leant forward.

'Well …'

'Are you ladies ready to order?'

Stella rolled her eyes at the waiter. 'Not now, Joe. She was just about to spill her guts.'

Stella was a regular. Joe knew she meant no offence.

'Then how about I bring you some olives and a bottle of Chardonnay to start with?' he suggested.

'Thanks. Sounds lovely,' said Stella, shooing him away with her hand.

He winked at Cara before heading back to the kitchen.

'You know he's dead keen on you,' hissed Stella in a failed whisper.

'Speaking of dead, my grandmother spoke to me from the grave,' said Cara, changing the subject. Joe was gorgeous, but not her type at all. She preferred tall and wiry over toned and tanned. She preferred Flynn.

'That doesn't sound like the beginning,' said Stella frowning.

Cara told the story in as much detail as she could before pulling the sunstone from the neckline of her shirt and dangling it from her fingertips.

'Oh, Cara. It's beautiful,' said Stella. 'Why haven't you worn it before?'

'I never realised how beautiful it was. I've only just had it cleaned. Bad granddaughter, I know.' She tucked it back in her shirt, wishing she had a cleavage like Stella's for it to nestle in. With her slim build, she was all angles instead of curves.

'Do you think it's working?' Stella asked. 'Joe did wink at you.'

'You know I don't like him that way,' she said, shaking her head.

'You don't like anyone that way.'

'That's not true!' She cursed herself for blurting out more than she intended.

'Then who?' pressed Stella, her eyes wide.

She hesitated, wanting to keep Flynn to herself for a moment more.

Stella rapped her fingernails on the table, getting impatient.

'Flynn,' said Cara, although it sounded more like an exhaling of breath than an actual name.

'Isn't he the one from the orphanage?' asked Stella, breaking into a smile.

'How did you remember that?'

Stella couldn't remember who the prime minister was yet she'd managed to retrieve that detail. She was unbelievable.

'I remember everything about you,' she said. *'Everything.'*

'Think I'm going to put you in that horror movie with my grandmother.' Cara's hair shimmied down her back as she laughed.

'But you told me you're just friends.' Stella's brows knitted together as she tried to piece together what Cara was telling her.

'I'm not sure if we're even that. I haven't spoken to him since I got back. Plus he lives in Perth. That's miles from Melbourne.'

'Fancy a girls' weekend in the wild west?'

The way Stella's eyes were twinkling made Cara's stomach churn with trepidation.

'I couldn't.'

'You absolutely could.' Stella reached across and gripped Cara's hands. 'Come on, we've talked about going away for ages. We could go this weekend.'

'But what if he's busy?' Her pulse rate rose. Stella was serious. And she made it sound so easy when it was intensely complicated.

'We'll have a blast anyway,' said Stella. 'We could go to a day spa. You need to look after yourself, remember?'

'But I need to get the girls ready for their exams. And I promised Mum I'd take her to the dentist on Friday.' The excuses in her mind didn't sound as solid when spoken aloud.

'Enough. This is exactly what Mary was telling you. You're too busy worrying about everyone else.'

'I suppose ...'

'Sold! It's locked in. We're going.' Stella's eyes burned with excitement as she clapped her hands.

'Isn't it short notice?' The trepidation churning in her stomach stepped up to a speed so high it threatened to turn into a solid lump of butter.

'What does your heart want?' asked Stella.

There was only one answer to that.

Flynn.

Maybe it was time to look after herself. The world could live without her for one weekend. Her students wouldn't fail their exams and her mother could find someone else to take her to the dentist.

She reached for her necklace and felt the warmth of the sunstone in her fingertips.

'Let's do it.'

She needn't have spoken. Stella was already on her phone looking up flights.

~ * ~

'Hello, Flynn, this is Cara, from the or—'

'Cara! It's so nice to hear from you. How are you?'

His voice sounded like honey. She could practically smell his aftershave down the phone, so clear was her memory of it.

'I'm good, thanks. Sorry to bother you.'

'You're not bothering me. I gave you my number for you to call me. It wasn't for you to pick lotto numbers with.'

She'd forgotten how funny he was. Not like some guys who tried too hard. It was his relaxed style that drew her in and made her smile.

'I'm coming to Perth this weekend and I was wondering if maybe you'd ... like to catch up or something?'

'That would be great. I just ... oh, yeah, no, that would be great.'

'You have plans, don't you?' She scrunched up her face, feeling like the world's biggest fool.

'Um, yeah, kind of. But don't worry. I'm changing them. It's only my brother. He'll understand.'

'I'll have a friend with me. Maybe we can all meet up? Then you don't have to change your plans.'

'Brilliant. Yes. Fantastic. A double date.'

'Who said anything about a date?'

'Me! I did. It's definitely a date. You one hundred percent just asked me out on a date and I said yes.'

She giggled. 'Oh, really.'

'Except for one problem ... '

'What's that?'

'My brother's married with three kids, so it's not really a double date. You'd better tell your friend.'

'I'm sure she'll cope. Should I give you a call on Saturday to organise where to meet?'

'Sounds good. I'm glad you called. Really, I am.'

'Me too.'

'I didn't think you would.'

'Me too.'

She lay back on her bed and smiled. It was the kind of smile that emanated from the deepest part of her heart and radiated to every nerve cell in her brain.

It was time for Cara to take care of Cara.

~ * ~

'I can't do it.' Cara grasped Stella's arm trying to pull her towards the bar's exit.

'Which one is he?' Stella said, ignoring her protest.

'The tall one in the blue shirt.'

Stella nodded. 'Nice. His brother's nice too. Pity about the brother's wife.'

'Sorry about that.'

'Next time I expect you to fall for someone with a single brother, okay?'

'Who said anything about falling?'

'Your face did. Look at you. Your jaw's practically on the floor.'

Cara closed her lips firmly. 'It is not.'

'Go and say hello,' said Stella, shoving her in Flynn's direction.

She took a deep breath, slightly disappointed that Flynn was as gorgeous as she'd remembered. Walking over to him would be much easier if he wasn't so attractive.

His face turned as if drawn to her by a magnetic force and he broke into a smile.

She smiled meekly in return as he stood up from his chair and closed the distance between them.

'Hi, Cara.'

'Hi.' The word came out more like a squeak.

He reached for her, drawing her to his chest.

Her arms instinctively wrapped around his waist in response. She remembered the chaste kiss on the cheek she'd given him when they'd said farewell in Sri Lanka. Compared to that, this embrace was practically X-rated.

'You look beautiful,' he whispered in her ear and she felt the warmth of his breath on her neck. The scent of him was intoxicating. It'd been a long time since she'd smelt pure male at such close proximity.

She could feel the sunstone digging into her chest. It was the most beautiful gift her grandmother could've given her. Not the stone itself, but what it had brought into her life—this gorgeous man with his arms around her, telling her she was beautiful.

It seemed her grandmother did love her after all.

Flynn released his embrace and placed a hand on each of her shoulders so he could look at her more closely. His blue eyes were sparkling, sending electricity flying between them.

'You've clearly been taking good care of yourself,' he said.

She laughed. 'Oh, if only you knew.'

She couldn't keep her heart protected forever. Happiness came with risks. It didn't matter if things worked out with Flynn for one day, one year or one lifetime.

Right now she was giving happiness a shot.

The Heart of Stone

By

Melanie Coles

Emmett Stone stood outside the jewellery store, his gloved fingers nervously playing with the small, velvet box in his pocket. For ten minutes he'd been glued to the footpath debating this next move. Three days ago—Christmas Eve, the night he'd had his epiphany—it had all seemed so clear and he'd spent the next thirty-six hours planning a course of action. Only now, standing here in the freezing cold about to enact said plan, he'd never been more nervous in his life.

Could he really pull this off?

'Get it together, Stone,' he muttered, tugging his scarf a little tighter. 'You broker million-dollar deals every day. How hard can this be?'

Drawing a deep breath, he pushed the door and stepped inside. A bell tinkled from somewhere above his head, announcing his entrance. 'Hello?' He closed the door and pulled off his gloves. The store appeared deserted. He headed towards the counter. 'Callie?'

Callie Reid, his best friend's sister and jeweller extraordinaire, appeared from a doorway to his right. 'Emmett?'

'Hi there.'

'Hi. This is a surprise.' She smiled and tucked a strand of honey-blonde hair behind her ear. 'Come to say goodbye?'

Goodbye? Parker hadn't mentioned anything about her leaving. 'I beg your pardon?'

'Before your trip?' She tilted her head slightly. 'You left so quickly the other night that I …' She stopped and cleared her throat. 'I, uh, thought Parker said you were heading to New York straight after Christmas.'

'Oh.' He breathed a sigh of relief. 'Something came up. I changed my plans.' He unwound his scarf. 'I wasn't sure you'd be open this late. Or this week, for that matter. Everyone else seems to be closed.' He indicated the empty stores outside.

'What can I say? I'm a workaholic with no social life.'

'That's something we have in common.'

That made her laugh. 'I guess so. What brings you by?'

'You.'

'Me?'

'Well, your expertise, actually.' He pulled the box from his pocket and placed it on the counter. 'I was hoping you could do something with this.' He pushed it towards her and waited.

Callie's eyes remained fixed on the box. 'What is it?'

Satisfied that he'd made the right decision, he smiled. 'Open it and see.'

~ * ~

Callie stared at the small black box for ages, trying to bring her breathing under control. It was crazy that being in the same room with Emmett still did this to her after all these years. Ever since that first day her brother Parker had brought him home to visit—when she was a gawky sixteen year old and he a strapping nineteen year old university student—she'd been unable to stop her emotional, often physical, reaction to his presence. And the lapse of ten years hadn't lessened it a jot. She was still as much in love with Emmett Stone as ever.

Not that he knew that.

Callie had mastered the art of concealment. Even after their recent Christmas Eve, under-the-mistletoe … *encounter,* she'd managed to act like it was nothing out of the ordinary. Like his arm around her waist and his lips pressed against hers hadn't ignited a raging fire of desire within her. Because no matter how much her body and soul wanted him, Callie knew it was nothing more to Emmett than a moment of alcohol-induced, Christmas festivity between friends.

And that's how it was going to stay.

Still, having him push a velvet ring box across the counter towards her was a little unnerving.

'Callie?' He was waiting for her to speak. 'Are you okay?'

'Yes. Sorry Emmett.' She shook her head to clear her thoughts and reached for the box. Opening the lid, she gasped. 'Oh my. Emmett, it's … it's beautiful.'

In all her years as a custom jeweller, it was the first time she'd come across a sunstone. She'd seen pictures, of course, in her many gemstone books and a few industry catalogues. The fact was that most people had never even heard of it, let alone put in a request for one. Rubies. Diamonds. Emeralds. Sapphires. These were the staples of her business. But there was something about the russet hues of this little-known gem—the earthy, natural tones—that appealed to Callie, both creatively and personally.

She reached for her loupe. 'Where did you get this?' she asked, putting the eyeglass in to examine the ring more closely.

'It's my mother's. And her mother's before that, I think.' Emmett leaned against the counter. 'But as you can see, some of the diamonds are missing.' He pointed to several gaps. 'And the setting is a little dated. I thought you could use the stone and what's left of the diamonds and design something new.'

Callie stilled, removed the loupe and stared at Emmett. 'You want me to design you a new ring?'

He nodded.

'What for?' The question tumbled out before she could stop herself. When Emmett raised a questioning eyebrow, she added hastily, 'What I mean is, do you intend it to be something to be worn every day? Because that would alter the kind of metal you'd use in the band.'

'Really? I didn't know that.' Emmett tapped a finger against his lips. 'Okay … well, I'd hazard a guess and say make it for everyday wear. But other than that, I'm happy for you take care of the design for me.'

'I don't know, Emmett.' Callie sucked in a breath before snapping the box lid shut and pushing it back towards him. 'That ring is a family heirloom and …'

'Please, Callie.' Emmett's warm hand covered hers, momentarily startling her and encasing the box within her palm. 'You are the most talented jeweller in London, and my best friend's sister. Plus, you know my mother. And me.' His eyes softened. 'I don't trust anyone else to do justice to this piece.'

She lost herself in the blue of his eyes and relented. 'Okay,' she said. 'I'll do it. But if your mother hates it …'

'She won't. I promise.' He held up two fingers in a scout salute.

'When do you need it by?'

Emmett released her hand and reached for his gloves. 'Mum's birthday party is on the eighteenth,' he said, pulling them on. 'Can you have it ready by then?'

Three weeks. It was tight, but …

'Fine,' she said. 'The eighteenth it is.'

~ * ~

Phase one now complete, Emmett drove to his mother's house, where he found her anxiously waiting for him.

'Well?' she asked, setting down her book as he walked into the sitting room. 'Did you give it to her? What did she say?'

Emmett hung his coat on the rack in the corner and sank into his favourite chair. 'Well, I had to break out some of the old Emmett charm, but she's going to do it,' he said, stretching his hands towards the fire. 'And she said she'd have it done by the eighteenth.'

'Wonderful.' His mother clapped her hands together. 'So that's done. What next?'

'Parker.'

'Oh.' She leaned back in her chair.

'I'm not sure how he's going to feel about this. He's always been protective of Callie.'

'You haven't spoken to him yet?'

Emmett shook his head. 'I didn't want to in case today's part of the plan went south. Parker would never forgive me if I screwed this up.'

The realisation that he'd fallen for his best friend's sister weighed heavily on Emmett. He'd always had a soft spot for her, but he'd put it down to not having any siblings of his own. She'd never been on his radar. But then Christmas Eve happened …

He wasn't even planning to go to Parker and Holly's annual Christmas Eve party, but guilt eventually forced him out of the office and into their living room, where at some point he'd found himself standing with Callie—both of them slightly tipsy—under the mistletoe. He wasn't sure who made the first move; just that her lips were suddenly touching his and his arm somehow wound its way around her waist. In that moment, Emmett's whole world shattered. No longer just his friend or his mate's baby sister, Callie Reid was all grown up.

And by God, if he didn't love her.

The shock of his discovery had him hightailing it out of there the first chance he got. Only later did he realise she'd kissed him back. It's what had finally convinced him to act.

'You've gone quiet, Emmett.'

He looked up to find his mother's gentle eyes assessing him. 'Sorry. Just thinking.'

'Second thoughts?'

'No.' There was no turning back now. He was in this. All the way. 'I've got to go,' he said, standing. He kissed her cheek. 'I'll call you tomorrow.'

'Good luck, love.'

As he headed out to his car, Emmett pulled out his phone and dialled.

'Parker? It's me. I'm coming over. You and I need to talk.'

Time for phase two.

~ * ~

'I swear, Holly. It's the most beautiful stone I've ever laid eyes on.' Callie brought up the photos she'd snapped on her phone earlier that day and leaned across the kitchen counter to show her sister-in-law. 'See? The colour is exquisite.'

'It *is* lovely,' Holly said, sipping her wine. 'But then you've always had a sweet spot for those rustic tones, Cal. I can see why it would appeal to you.' Stirring the risotto, she asked, 'Do you know what you're planning to do with it?'

'I've got some ideas.' Callie had been sketching all afternoon, design after design flowing from the tip of her pencil. She'd been so engrossed that she'd almost forgotten about dinner at Parker and Holly's.

She put her phone away and cradled her wine glass with both hands. 'I still can't believe Emmett gave me free reign on this design. Usually when I get jobs there's a brief as long as my arm.'

'Of course he'd give you free reign, Cal. You're the best jewellery designer in the whole freaking country.' Holly held up her left hand as proof. 'Not to mention that Parker would beat him senseless if he used someone else.'

'Not over jewellery, I wouldn't.' Parker entered the kitchen and pulled a beer from the fridge. Loosening his tie, he flicked the top two buttons on his shirt, popped the lid on his bottle and pulled. 'Emmett and I may have been friends since university,' he said, wiping his mouth with the back of his hand, 'but if he dared to hurt anyone I love, then, hell yeah, I'd beat him senseless.' As if to prove he was serious he added, 'And then I'd feed his balls to Monty.'

Callie glanced at the terrier lying serenely on a mat in the corner and laughed. 'It's a good thing for Emmett, then, that he's only after me for my incredible design skills, eh?'

A look passed between husband and wife before Holly quickly turned off the hob. 'This is ready,' she said, lifting the pot off the stove and delivering it to the table. 'Let's eat, shall we?'

After they'd finished and were onto their second bottle of wine, Callie said, 'I got my invitation to Emmett's mum's birthday party today.' Alice Stone's parties had been an annual fixture on their calendar for as long as they'd known Emmett.

Holly squealed. 'Us too! And did you see where they're holding it? *Swoon.*'

The upmarket establishment in Camden was equal parts rustic and elegance. Callie had been there once and absolutely adored it. 'I know. Emmett sure is going all out this year.'

'Of course he is.' Parker leaned back in his chair. 'It's Alice's sixtieth.'

'I know. I know. But it's after five wear,' Callie said, sighing. 'Which counts out practically everything in my current wardrobe.'

'So, we'll go shopping tomorrow,' Holly said. 'I'll pick you up at three. There's a great new boutique in Notting Hill that stocks the most amazing dresses. In fact,' she squeezed Callie's arm. 'We'll both find something new. Okay?'

Parker groaned and collected their dishes, muttering something about overtime and next month's credit card bill as he headed for the kitchen.

~ * ~

It was four in the afternoon and the light was just beginning to fade as Emmett stood at his office window, hands in pockets, staring out across the city. In a little over four hours, he'd put the final phase of his plan into action. Phase one had been easy. Phase two had been … well, a little more difficult. Parker had needed persuading, but Emmett had found a willing ally in Holly, thank God. But phase three …

Phase three was high risk.

Taking risks was nothing new to Emmett. It's what made him a successful businessman, but never had the stakes been so high. So personal. Because he was placing his most valuable commodity on the line.

His heart.

He was about to take the biggest gamble of his life. He just hoped to God it would pay off.

~ * ~

Stepping out of the taxi, Callie tucked her purse under her arm while she adjusted her dress, the delicate bronze chiffon rippling under her fingertips. Holly sure had a great eye for fashion; Callie felt every bit the princess. Satisfied she wasn't going to trip on the hem with her heels, she made her way inside.

The party was already in full swing. Callie checked her coat and then scanned the crowd. She spotted Holly and Parker sitting at a corner table and started to make her way there, when …

'There you are.'

Emmett.

Mentally preparing—yet again—to fight her body's response to him, Callie turned … and for the first time in a decade knew she was going to fail. Emmett always looked sharp, but tonight—in a charcoal suit and deep blue tie that matched his eyes—he was devastating. As her heart began turning cartwheels in her chest, it took all of her concentration just to remain coherent. 'H-hello Emmett.'

'You look beautiful tonight.'

The unexpected compliment coloured her cheeks. 'Thank you. This place is amazing.' She loved the exposed brickwork and polished wooden furniture, but it was the fairy lights strung across the length of the room and the tea light candles flickering on the tables that created a magical effect. 'It's the perfect place for this event.'

'I thought so.' He led her to a corner of the room away from the main crowd. 'You've brought it?'

Opening her purse, she withdrew the velvet box. 'Here it is,' she said, holding it out to him. 'I really hope she'll like it, Emmett.'

She held her breath while he opened it, wondering what he'd think of her design. She'd used rose gold for the setting and, drawing inspiration from the sun, surrounded the main stone with delicate swirls, which she'd then dotted with the remaining diamonds. It was far and away her best work. 'Well? What do you think?'

She heard his intake of breath as he stared at the glistening piece. 'Callie, it's stunning.'

'Do you think so?'

'Absolutely.' He examined it more closely. 'But … I don't think it's the right piece for mum.'

Her heart sank. 'You don't?'

'No. It looks more like something a man would give to the woman he loves.'

'Oh.' The thought hadn't occurred to Callie, but looking at it more closely, she could see his point. 'I suppose it does, doesn't it?' She touched his arm lightly. 'I'm so sorry, Emmett.'

'Why? You filled the brief perfectly.'

'Perfectly?' She laughed. 'I made you an engagement ring, Emmett.'

'Which I fully intend to make use of, Callie. If you'll have me, that is.'

It took a moment for his words to register, and another to realise he'd closed the gap between them to mere centimetres. All the air in her lungs froze and his eyes—so intense—held her like a deer caught in headlights. 'W-w-what did you say?'

'Callie.' He smiled, his voice a caress. 'For ten years you've been right there in front of me, but it took that kiss under the mistletoe to make me see it. To make me see *you*.' His fingers grazed her cheek. 'I've been hoping to win your heart ever since.'

She had to be dreaming. He … he loved her?

'Tell me. Do you think I have a chance?' He reached for her hand. 'Because I love you, Callie. With all of my heart.'

He did. He really loved her. Emmett Stone. Loved. Her.

Oh God. She was going to cry. Right there in front of him.

She nodded through her tears and he smiled. Retrieving the ring from the box, Emmett held it before her. 'The sunstone in this ring has been in our family for three generations, given as a symbol of love. First to my grandmother, then my mother, who passed it on to me. Now, I'm offering it to you.' He lowered himself to one knee. 'Callie Reid, will you marry me?'

His words released the yoke Callie had kept tightly wound around her feelings.

'Yes.' She held out her left hand and let him slip the ring on her finger. 'Yes, Emmett Stone. I will marry you.'

The room erupted in applause as Emmett stood. They both turned. Every guest was cheering; Parker, Holly and Alice Stone the loudest of all.

Callie looked at Emmett. 'They knew, didn't they?'

'They did.' He grinned and wrapped his arms around her waist. 'You think I could propose to you without clearing it with Parker first? He'd have pummelled me to death.'

'But your mum … this is her night and … oh dear.' She held up her hand, where the sunstone ring now graced her finger. 'This was her birthday gift, Emmett.'

'Trust me,' he said, pulling her close. 'She's received the only present she wanted.' He touched his forehead to hers. 'A soon-to-be daughter-in-law.'

'But Emmett …'

He stopped her objection with a kiss. A real one. Without the mistletoe. And she was more than happy to kiss him back.

She loved him.

And she didn't care who knew.

Follow Your Dreams

By

Fiona Greene

'I thought I'd find you here.'

Riley Ellison's heart stopped, then raced into overdrive. She'd have known that voice anywhere. 'Mark?' She turned, loosening her grip on the rail, but not letting go. 'Mark Stewart?'

It was, but it wasn't.

Mark's sun-bleached bad-boy locks were history, replaced by a close crop with a touch of grey at the temples but it was the eyes that gave him away. The same ice-blue pools she'd always found fascinating.

'Who else?' Mark's smile didn't quite reach his eyes. 'Riley, you haven't changed a bit. You're even wearing the sunstone.'

Riley clutched at the pendant. 'Am I so predictable?' Truth be told, she was having trouble talking. Mark Stewart, circa 2016, was hot. The rangy teen with the freckles and the skinny jeans was all grown up. Beefed up, too, she thought as she checked out Mark's shoulders under his well-cut jacket.

Matured, she decided, trying to get her wayward thoughts under control.

'Deanna gave you that pendant. She ordered it from Sunstone's fan club.'

'I'm surprised you remember.'

Mark finally smiled. 'How could I forget? She paid it off in instalments using my credit card.' He dropped his eyes. 'It was supposed to be for your eighteenth birthday, but she was so excited she gave it to you months early. On the day of the last Sunstone concert here at the Entertainment Centre.'

They both fell silent as they remembered.

Riley snuck a look under her fringe and saw the man she'd loved since she was fourteen.

What did Mark see?

His dead sister's best friend?

Or someone who ran when the going got tough?

~ * ~

The last traces of the reflected sunset disappeared from the lake next to the Entertainment Centre and Riley's skin crawled. The last time she'd been here, fat raindrops had churned the water and the red and blue lights of the emergency services had stolen the darkness.

Tonight, it was clear. The formal lawn that sloped down from the forecourt to the water's edge was dotted with picnic rugs with concert-goers choosing an early arrival and twilight picnic, instead of wrestling the parking queues closer to show time.

Over in the beer garden, diehard rock fans in jeans and faded Sunstone T-shirts caught up over beer and burgers. Once upon a time, that would have been her.

Twenty-five years had passed since the last time she'd stood on this boardwalk. Time enough for two careers, three relationships, one cat and more guilt than she cared to remember.

She rubbed at the goose bumps on her arms.

What did you say to the man who'd been your first? When you hadn't seen him since? The words she'd rehearsed so many times, 'Mark, it's great to see you,' remained stuck as her throat squeezed tight. Instead she took a deep breath and blurted, 'I'm sorry. I should never have given Deanna your keys.'

Mark's breath whistled out between his teeth. 'I'm the one who should be sorry. I shouldn't have told her to wait in the car.'

'After … I wanted to call.' Riley swallowed hard. 'But I couldn't.'

'Couldn't, or didn't want to?'

Mark's words cut her to the quick. So many nights she'd tossed and turned, her thoughts filled with the man beside her. Wanting to pick up the phone, but petrified her father would make good his threat of laying charges against bad boy Mark Stewart for touching his underage daughter.

'Couldn't,' she whispered. 'My actions, our actions, had already stolen one child from your family. I couldn't let them lock you up. That's what my parents said the police would do if I contacted you.'

Mark shifted his feet. 'When I heard Sunstone was coming back to town …' he trailed off.

Riley nodded. 'Me too. I had to come.'

Mark gestured to the wooden structure up the slope. 'We should walk.'

Riley took a deep breath. She hadn't looked at the historic wedding chapel she knew lay preserved forever in the tranquil gardens. She didn't want to see the tiny bronze plaque in the rose garden.

Didn't want to remember.

She gave herself a mental shake. She was going to keep the promise she'd made to herself this morning as she'd fastened Deanna's pendant around her neck.

It was time.

They left the boardwalk and crossed the lawn. Riley stumbled as her heels sunk into the grass and Mark reached out to steady her. His touch sent tingles shooting up her arm.

'Riley, I wanted to see you.' Mark's words were rushed. 'I wanted to be with you. We never even got to talk.'

'No,' Riley agreed, remembering the gut-wrenching fear that had crippled her when Deanna hadn't met up with them as planned. Then, the second her heart stopped when she realised it was Mark's hatchback submerged in the ornamental lake. The car Deanna had the keys to.

As Deanna's body had been retrieved, she and Mark had been put in separate police cars, and grilled repeatedly. 'My parents, they couldn't cope with what I'd done. They ran.' Riley tried to smile. 'Even now, they can't face what happened.'

'I know. The day of the inquest, Dad had a stroke, and Mum still blames me.' Mark rubbed his brow. 'They can't let it go.'

Riley stared into the distance and rubbed at the tight spot in her chest. 'I continually disappoint. Especially now that I'm single again and there aren't any grandkids pending.'

'Oh, I hear you.' Pain lanced across Mark's face. 'Mum's worn out. I offer to help, but …'

'I know. One stupid teenage mistake and they don't trust you for the rest of your life.'

'A mistake?'

Riley looked up into Mark's eyes. 'Wrong choice of word. *They* call it the mistake that ruined my life.'

Mark leaned towards her. 'And you?'

'The best day of my life, the worst day of my life. That night, you opened a door for me and gave me a glimpse of a future, meaningful and alive. And then it was slammed shut in my face.' Riley's words tumbled out on a shaky breath. 'It took me a long time to move forward. I've always felt guilty because sometimes, instead of mourning Deanna, I was mourning what I'd lost.' She stopped and Mark stopped with her. 'What we'd lost.'

Riley leaned into Mark, stunned at how right it felt being with him. As though their time apart had never happened.

Mark reached out to brush Riley's hair from her face. 'Everyone's life changed forever that night. Mine went from mediocre, to fabulous, to downright horrific, all within four hours. And nobody was going to allow me to mourn what I'd lost.'

Riley's breath left her in a shuddery sob. Mark's life had directly mimicked hers. 'I've never visited before,' she confessed, heart pounding. 'I just couldn't.'

'It took me a long time to be comfortable here. At first, all I could see was the horror. As time passed, it became special, a place that's mine and Deanna's, where I can remember her the way I want.'

They started walking again, toward the chapel.

Riley nodded. 'I like that.' How much easier would it have been if she'd had the opportunity to mourn Deanna in her own way, her own time?

'Round there, to the left.' Mark ushered Riley onto the crushed gravel path.

She saw the plaque immediately, bathed in the gentle glow of the up-lights. She swallowed hard then stepped up to the memorial.

Deanna Irene Stewart–Ever Remembered–1976–1991.

Her hands shook as she eased a spray of miniature white roses from her bag. She'd bought them earlier, not even sure she'd be brave enough to come.

Had she known Mark would be here?

The only person on the planet who truly understood her pain.

Was that why she'd been compelled to buy them?

Because her heart had known he'd be here to support her?

She knelt down, brushed the dust from the plaque and laid the tiny bouquet.

'Let's take a moment to remember.' Mark's voice was gravelly. 'For Deanna.'

'For Deanna,' she repeated.

Mark offered his hand and Riley grasped it to stand. His fingers were warm and comforting. He didn't let go, instead rubbing his thumb slowly over the back of her hand. They stood shoulder to shoulder and Riley glanced up at the man her first boyfriend had become. The man who'd haunted her all these years.

Mark squeezed her fingers.

Riley squeezed back.

~ * ~

How long they stayed like that, Riley didn't know. She surfaced from her memories to the sound of the fifteen-minute chimes. 'We should go.'

She sensed, rather than saw Mark's nod.

'Thanks for coming with me. I'm not sure I would have braved it on my own.'

Mark kept hold of her fingers as they walked. 'I know how hard it is. I didn't deal with it to start with. It wasn't until I went to counselling with my ex, that I admitted that.'

Riley pulled her hand away as though she'd been burnt. 'You got married?'

Mark wasn't hers, hadn't ever really been hers, but the thought of him married, with children, tore another hole in her already shattered heart.

'Was married.' Mark's face was grim. 'Not because I loved her. Not because I wanted to. I thought it was the right thing to do. Stupidly, I tried to replace the happy family we'd lost; to give my parents the grandchildren they so desperately wanted.' He paused. 'At least Adele came to her senses before we had any kids.'

Riley stopped walking. 'Not Adele Peterson?'

Mark closed his eyes and nodded.

She winced at the thought of bad boy Mark Stewart with straight laced, uniforms below the knee, A-grade student Adele Peterson. 'No offence, but I could have told you that would never work.'

'It wasn't about me. I tried everything to make Mum smile again.'

'And did she?'

'For a while, but my heart wasn't in it. I couldn't go on living the lie. It wasn't fair on Adele.'

Anger built in Riley's chest. She'd missed all this. Torn away in a cloud of shame to start her life over. Far from the scandal and the temptation of that wicked, wicked Mark Stewart.

'That must have been hard. I disappointed everyone in my family, but at least there wasn't a yawning hole at the dinner table to remind everyone of my indiscretion.' Riley reached for Mark's hand again. 'Not that that's how I thought of it.'

Mark's gaze smouldered as he linked his fingers with hers. 'How did you think of it?'

'Best night of my life.' Riley flashed him a shy smile. 'Right up to the bit where Deanna didn't meet up with us as planned.'

'Yeah.' Mark stared off into the distance. 'Yeah.'

He looked so sad, so lost, that her heart broke. 'Best night of my life,' she whispered.

~ * ~

The warning chimes sounded again. Mark kept a firm grip on Riley's hand as they joined the steady stream of people walking up the path to the concert arena. Now that he'd found Riley, he didn't want to let her go. 'I'll walk with you to your gate.'

'No, it's fine.'

'I want to. Which gate?' The incoming crowd jostled against them so Mark steered them off to one side and held out his hand for Riley's ticket. 'Gate four.'

'Where are you?'

'Nineteen. The opposite side of the arena.' Mark screwed his face up. 'Story of our lives, right?'

'I guess.'

Mark's stomach dropped as his feeble attempt at a joke fell flat. Did Riley think he was talking about the past, or the future? 'Come on.' He pulled Riley into the crush of people. 'We might not be able to sit together but we're not missing out on Sunstone live. Not this time.' He'd ruined it for Riley last time. This was his chance to make amends.

'Okay.' Riley's brown eyes were clouded in confusion.

Hell.

Was Riley slipping away from him?

The spark was still there and they'd seemed so close down at the chapel. Their years apart had evaporated and he'd been ecstatic. Now, his gut was churning.

Was she regretting his approach?

No. Riley had been genuinely pleased to see him. A little shocked. But pleased. More likely, she'd started to think through the repercussions of them reconnecting. Riley re-introducing Mark to her family. Mark doing the same. Both of them busting a gut to please everyone but themselves.

So much had changed since he'd last seen her, but he knew one thing for certain. He was going to do his damnedest not to lose Riley Ellison again.

She was beautiful.

Sure, there was pain in her eyes, but if anything, that made her even more gorgeous. After all this time, he still wanted to grow old with Riley.

Warmth pooled in his belly. And lower, he thought grimly.

So what are you going do about it?

Let her go?

Again?

Mark tightened his grip on Riley's hand and together they weaved their way through the crowd. He stopped just short of her gate, surprising Riley, who ploughed into him. The brief contact electrified him. 'Sorry about that. You okay?'

'Yep.'

Mark pulled his mobile from his pocket. 'Five minutes till show time. Just enough time for you to give me your number.'

Riley stared up at him, eyes wide. 'You want my number?'

'I wouldn't have asked for it otherwise. We could get a drink after the show?'

Riley's face lit up. The first genuine smile Mark had seen all evening. 'I'd love to.' She rattled off her number.

Mark sent her a blank text. 'There,' he said when Riley's phone beeped. 'You've got my number. I'll meet you here.' He brushed Riley's forehead with his lips. 'See you then.'

The foyer was deserted as Mark jogged back around the arena to his gate. He grinned and resisted the urge to punch the air.

For once in his life, he'd made the right choice.

~ * ~

One message received.

As the lights in the arena dimmed, Riley's phone shone like a beacon in her lap.

What on earth was she going to do?

Her heart yelled yes, but her head screamed no.

In her mother's voice.

Her thumb hovered. She could delete Mark's number with one quick push. March out of here right now and keep travelling down the path her parents had forced her onto all those years ago.

Or you could choose to move forward.

She peered out into the gloom, trying to find Mark across the massive expanse of the arena. Hopeless, she decided, as the house lights went down. An expectant silence settled over the crowd.

Be here now.

She focused on her breathing as the familiar riff of Sunstone's signature anthem broke the silence, and in a sweep of lights the stage came to life.

Instantly, she was transported back twenty-five years—a carefree teenager who only cared about saving enough pocket money to buy the next album from the rock band in front of her. The set finished with the haunting drums of *Take What You Can Get* echoing away to nothing and the stage lights faded. Screams and applause echoed in the darkness.

As silence engulfed the arena, a thick beam of orange illuminated the stage. Gabriella, Sunstone's lead singer, her fiery orange curls now styled in a sleek bob, perched on a stool, guitar on her lap.

Riley leaned forward in anticipation.

'I was last here a quarter of a century ago and I'm not sure how many of you were.' A few of the fans whooped and cheered. 'That show's always stayed with me. One of my young fans died in a horrific accident, right here at this arena.' Her voice cracked and she sipped some water. The crowd was silent. 'I wrote this next song at the end of that tour. I've never released it, or performed it in front of an audience before, but when I knew I was coming back down under, I …' She trailed off and sipped her water again. 'The song's called *Lost*, and this one's for Deanna.'

Gabriella closed her eyes and strummed her guitar. The audience stayed silent, mesmerised as she sang the story of young lovers who snuck away before a rock concert to be together, but who paid the ultimate sacrifice when the their young charge died on their watch.

Shivers ran up Riley's spine as she listened to the final refrain.

Their love, it was forbidden,

Futures torn apart.
Consequences far-reaching,
Like ripples on a pond.
Lost.
Lost.

~ * ~

Riley sat back, desperately trying to draw breath.

It was their story.

Hers and Mark's.

She reached for her pendant, her fingertip tracing the stone.

Gabriella played the final chords. The crowd was silent for all of ten seconds, then they erupted. Gabriella stayed centre stage, listening to the relentless cheers and whistles. When the applause died down, she spoke. 'Thank you. I'm glad you liked it. I'm hoping those young lovers are here somewhere tonight. And if you are, I hope you followed your dreams and found happiness together.'

Riley's phone fell from her lap unheeded as she swallowed back her tears. It was so surreal, her idol telling *their* story.

And, most importantly, giving it a happy ending.

Something Riley had never been able to do.

On the floor, her phone flashed an incoming message. Hands shaking, she snatched it up and opened the message.

Are you ready to follow your dreams and find happiness with me?

Riley's heart thumped as she stared at the screen.

Could she keep the promise she'd made to herself this morning? Leave the emptiness behind, and move forward?

Riley held the sunstone, took a deep breath and closed her eyes.

Seconds later, they flicked open.

Happiness bubbled up in her chest.

Her thumbs flew over the keypad.

With you, Mark, only with you.

Breaking Free

By

Monique Hall

Rachael breathed a sigh of relief when the taxi finally turned off the highway onto a sealed drive edged with grapevines. She moved to the edge of her seat and opened her window, letting the warm breeze breathe life back into her limp locks. Hooking her arms through the window and sticking her head out into the bright California sunshine, she was unable to hide the grin that demanded to make itself known. Who knew that something as simple as a journey's end could brighten her day? Or perhaps it was anticipation at seeing Corrine again.

They rounded a bend and her jaw dropped, a look of awe replacing her carefree grin, when an enormous Tuscan-inspired villa rose up out of the Santa Ynez Mountains. The cream limestone walls provided a subtle backdrop to the viridescent grapevines that seemed to pave the way and pay homage to their master. She knew Corrine's fiancé was a winemaker but she never could have imagined her best friend was about to become mistress of an estate this magnificent.

Corrine was waiting in welcome as the taxi rolled to a stop, a tall dark-haired man by her side, and although she'd never met him, Rachael recognised him from photos her best friend posted online.

Rachael leapt from the car, eager to see her friend for the first time in nearly two years. Squealing ensued as the two women wrapped each other in hugs and tears.

'I've missed you so much!'

'I can't believe you're finally here!'

'I know! It's been too long.'

'How was the flight?'

The sound of tyres crunching on gravel caught Rachael's attention. Her taxi was leaving and their dark-haired companion was putting his wallet away, Rachael's bags at his feet.

'Oh, you didn't need to …'

'Don't sweat it. Any friend of Corrine's is a friend of mine.' His welcoming grin transformed his chiselled features.

Rachael was amazed that she'd even noticed; it had been a long time since she'd found herself attracted to a man. It was a good thing that this one was off limits. She was definitely not in the market for a relationship.

'Rachael,' announced Corrine, 'meet my fiancé, Paul.'

'Nice to meet you, Rachael.' Paul moved forward and officially greeted Rachael with a warm shake of the hands and a polite peck on both cheeks, his good looks in such close proximity momentarily stunning her.

'Uh, likewise. Thanks for having me here.'

'Don't be silly,' said Corrine. 'There's no way I'd get married without my best friend to stand beside me. Now …' She grabbed Rachael by the shoulders and turned her so she was facing the architectural masterpiece that stood before them.

'Welcome to Sunstone Estate!'

The entrance was beautiful. The grand timber front doors were arched and edged with exquisitely carved limestone, and greenery crept up and over the porch. Pretty white flower arrangements sat perched on expertly crafted wine barrels, welcoming anyone privileged enough to approach the building. A shiver ran through

Rachael's body and her fingertips tingled. There was something special about this place. She could feel it.

Just as she was about to share these complimentary thoughts with her hosts, the front door opened and the breath was stolen from her lungs. Out stepped a truly glorious individual. He had to be related to Paul, whom she knew was of Italian descent, as he had the same dark hair and olive skin. She could quite easily picture him in a toga and sandals, all toned, tanned legs and bulging muscles.

She shook the images away as Corrine introduced them.

'Rach, this is Nick, Paul's cousin. He's originally from Oz too, so you guys have something in common. In fact, he's also the best man.'

Rachael made a noise of assent before she realised Corrine was referring to his role in the wedding. She blushed. Damn jet lag had her acting without thinking.

'It's a pleasure,' Nick's deep voice rumbled, his breath tickling the back of her hand as he kissed it.

Taken off guard, Rachael squeaked incoherently, nearly melting into a puddle on the floor as Nick's chocolate brown eyes twinkled.

Corrine cleared her throat, effectively breaking the spell. 'C'mon, Rach, we're a long way from Sydney. You probably need some rest.' Rachael was grateful when Corrine finally pulled her up onto the porch, preventing any further embarrassment.

In a moment of weakness she glanced over her shoulder only to see a knowing grin flashed in her direction as Nick's eyes locked onto her own. She frowned, trying to ignore the fluttering of butterflies that tickled her insides. She had not travelled half way around the world to take unnecessary risks. She was here for her friend's wedding and that was it.

~ * ~

'So the chemistry was sizzling down there!'

Corrine guided Rachael into one of the many guest rooms and closed the door, allowing them some privacy.

Rachael collapsed onto the enormous bed in the middle of the room. After the excitement of her arrival and subsequent introductions, her energy was spent.

'I don't know what you're talking about,' she breathed.

It might have been a while since the two women had been on the same continent, but they'd been best friends since kindergarten and they spoke regularly on Skype. Corrine knew all there was to know about Rachael.

'Don't ignore it, Rach. It's been twelve months. You need to get back out there. Take risks, live a little.'

'I'm not ready, C.'

The two friends considered each other for a moment before Corrine finally took pity on Rachael.

'Okay. We'll talk later after you've rested,' she said, bending to kiss Rachael's forehead. 'But just so you know, Darren didn't deserve you.'

Corrine left, leaving Rachael to curse the fact that it could still hurt, even after all this time.

~ * ~

After showering and sleeping half the day away, Rachael descended the staircase, following the sound of cheerful chatter and clinking cutlery. She emerged from the villa onto a patio overlooking the mountains and a magical golden sunset. She sucked in a breath, momentarily distracted by the beauty of the vista, before noticing a long table overladen with food, wine and glowing candles and surrounded by dinner guests. Several glanced in her direction before Corrine bounded over, a merry chorus greeting her as she was pushed into an empty seat and her wine glass was filled, the din rising as people turned back to their conversations.

'Glad you could join us.'

Rachael shivered involuntarily and she hesitated a moment before turning to acknowledge the speaker. Brown eyes regarded her with a mixture of heat and amusement, causing her to squirm in her seat.

'Is that so?' She averted her eyes and surveyed the feast spread out before them, doing her best to appear disinterested and aloof, all the while mentally cursing Corrine for placing her next to the one person she really didn't want to be seated with.

'Yeah, I need your opinion.' Nick leaned back, his legs sprawled out before him and an arm stretched across the back of her chair. He lifted his eyes to hers and smirked, oozing self-confidence.

Rachael appraised him and considered whether she should take the bait. Ignoring him wouldn't help anyone. They were both in the bridal party, after all; they had to get along. For Corrine's sake.

She settled for nonchalance instead. 'My opinion on what?' she sighed, avoiding eye contact as she spooned a serving of delicious-looking pasta onto her plate.

He leaned forward, invading her personal space and spoke close to her ear. 'On whether Corrine is the right woman for my cousin.'

That got her attention.

Rachael locked eyes with Nick, the hand holding the serving spoon frozen halfway between her plate and the bowl of pasta. Although he'd spoken quietly enough that only she had managed to pick up his disturbing comment, it didn't stop her from glancing nervously around to see if anyone had heard him.

Was he for real? Her best friend and his cousin were getting married in less than a week and he chose now to bring his concerns to the table? She lowered the serving spoon and turned toward him.

'What are you talking about?' she hissed. 'They're perfect for each other.' Okay, so maybe she'd only met Paul briefly this morning, but she knew her best friend and she'd watched them fall in love via Corrine's social media posts when her friend had first travelled to the States two years ago. She was deeply in love with him. Of course they were right for each other.

'I'm talking about the fact that they have nothing in common. How are they going to manage spending the rest of their lives together with nothing to talk about?' Nick remained calm despite the fact he was calling into question the happy couple's relationship. Meanwhile, Rachael's blood was beginning to boil.

'That's their business, not yours!'

'I'm just looking out for him. I don't want to see him make the biggest mistake of his life.'

'He's a big boy; I'm sure he knows what he's doing.'

'Maybe he's blinded by what's in front of him.'

'What's that supposed to mean?'

'It means that maybe he can't see Corrine's true motivation for being with him.'

Rachael's mouth dropped open. She was indignant on her friend's behalf. 'Are you saying she's with him for his money?'

'Hey, I'm just putting it out there.'

Rachael was speechless. She wanted to slap the smug look from his face, but instead they stared at each other in a silent stand-off.

A throat was cleared nearby.

Rachael's head snapped up. Everyone was looking at them.

'Everything okay over there?' asked Corrine, her brow creased with concern.

'Uh, s-sure,' Rachael stammered. Hell would freeze over before she ruined this wedding.

'Yeah, we were just discussing the merits of Sydney versus Melbourne. Rach got a little defensive about her home town, that's all.' Nick picked up his wine glass and aimed a smarmy grin in her direction.

She narrowed her eyes while everyone else accepted his explanation without question and went back to what they were doing.

'This conversation is not over!' she hissed.

He laughed. 'Thank goodness, I was thoroughly enjoying myself.' He turned from her then and struck up a good-natured conversation with Corrine's parents who were seated across the table.

Rachael sat fuming through the rest of the meal, plotting a way to convince Nick to drop his ridiculous notions about Paul and Corrine's compatibility.

~ * ~

After dinner, Rachael was given a tour around the villa—a good thing considering she was at risk of getting lost in the maze of never-ending rooms—but she was anxious to corner Nick and sort out his misguided opinion of her best friend once and for all.

'So,' said Corrine as she finished showing Rachael the last luxurious sitting room, 'what on earth went on between you and Nick during dinner? I know he was making excuses for some reason; you love Melbourne!'

'Ugh, he's so full of himself!' Rachael stalled for time.

Corrine looked at her as if she'd grown another head. 'I'd say I know Nick pretty well and that's definitely not how I'd describe him. What was he saying?'

Rachael bit her bottom lip. 'Nothing. He just doesn't know what he's talking about.'

'R-i-i-i-ght,' said Corrine, drawing the word out like she didn't believe a word Rachael was saying. 'Anyway, now that you're rested, I wanted to carry on our conversation from earlier. You've got me worried.'

'About what?'

Rachael knew exactly what Corrine was talking about. It had been a year since Darren had dumped her after three years together. Rachael hadn't seen it coming. She'd thought they'd be together forever; that they'd raise a family and grow old together. Instead, he'd given her excuses about wanting freedom and adventure and then took off to Europe without a backward glance, leaving her feeling abandoned and worthless. She'd been too scared to get close to anyone since. She couldn't risk another broken heart. It hurt too damn much.

'You know what I'm talking about, Rach.' Corrine pulled Rachael down onto a brown leather couch, her eyes full of pity. 'You don't go out, you don't socialise. You work, eat and sleep and that's it. You need to start living again.'

'I know,' whispered Rachael.

If arriving here in this majestic part of the world and her argument with Nick had shown her anything, it was that it felt good to feel something other than self-pity and resentment for a change. The beauty of Sunstone Estate made her feel content; it gave her hope that maybe she was finally ready to move on with her life.

Arguing with Nick, on the other hand, made her feel alive. It got the blood coursing through her veins and her body tingling with anticipation—whether for a fight or something else entirely, she wasn't quite sure.

'Oh … well, good,' said Corrine, clearly surprised she hadn't needed to be more persuasive. She then excused herself, claiming exhaustion, and reminded Rachael that she shouldn't stay up too long either if she hoped to adjust to the new time zone.

But Rachael had no intention of heading to bed anytime soon. She needed to find Nick and give him a piece of her mind.

He was still out on the patio, chatting to his aunt and uncle. When he saw her, he excused himself and indicated that she should walk with him. He casually lead the way along the length of the patio, making it appear as if they were taking a stroll, before grabbing her by the hand and pulling her down a row of grapevines.

Rachael held her tongue until they were far enough away from the others still on the patio, before yanking her hand from his grasp and pointing an accusing finger.

'How dare you insinuate that Corrine is a gold digger. She's welcomed you into her home and here you are, planning to ruin her wedding!' Rachael punctuated her last three words by jabbing her finger into Nick's shoulder. She couldn't help it—his amused grin was getting her riled up.

Nick didn't budge, but looked laughingly down at her, letting her get in his space, his eyes darkening a fraction despite reflecting the sparkling lights from the patio. Rachael regretted her actions immediately, something shifting in the tension between them when Nick grabbed her hand and pulled her up against him. His eyes flicked to her mouth before meeting her gaze once more.

'First of all, sweetheart, Sunstone Estate has been in my family for three generations; I'll always be welcome here.' He placed a finger to her lips when she tried to protest his arrogance. 'Secondly,' he looked at her pointedly, ensuring she was listening. 'Secondly, I've never been remotely close to thinking Corrine is anything but completely and utterly in love with my cousin; they belong together. It's obvious to everyone they meet.'

'Then what …?' Nick shushed her again, this time pressing a thumb firmly to her lips and cupping her cheek, effectively shocking her into submission.

'You were giving me the cold shoulder and I wanted to get under your skin. After the way you were blushing when we met this morning, there was no way in hell I was going to let you get away that easily.'

His voice dropped an octave and had grown husky. Rubbing his thumb across her lips, he lowered his mouth to hers and kissed her.

Rachael froze momentarily as she tried to decide whether or not to protest, but as she stood in Nick's embrace, the last twelve months of self deprecation and worthlessness melted away and something else took root—a hopeful kind of energy. It felt strange and unfamiliar but entirely welcome. She rose onto her toes and wound her arms around his shoulders as the lights from the villa shone its approval upon them.

~ * ~

Days later, Corrine and Paul became husband and wife and celebrated with their family and friends in the grounds of the estate with flowers, fairy lights and music creating an atmosphere that again proved to Rachael that this truly was a magical place, no doubt made all the more so with Nick by her side.

On her flight back to Sydney, Rachael opened her inflight magazine to find an article on the health benefits of Oregon sunstone. Seeing the connection with the place she'd found happiness and healing, she began reading.

Sunstone is believed to have many health benefits. As well as physical healing, the gem can also bring emotional healing to any who wear it, particularly those who experience feelings of abandonment and unworthiness. Sunstone will allow the wearer to break free from the bonds of fear and self-doubt by bringing balance to emotional patterns.

Rachael smiled. It was like she was reading about her own emotional journey of the last few weeks. Her time at Sunstone Estate had allowed her to experience life again, to see her own sense of value, and to help her realise that sometimes risks were worth taking.

And it had brought her to Nick.

For the first time in a long time, she had hope for the future. In a month, Nick would be joining her in Sydney. Not only would he be bringing Sunstone Estate's wines to the Australian market, but they would also have a chance to explore their relationship. She was finally free of the past.

~ * ~

When Nick proposed a year later on the steps of the Sydney Opera House, Rachael wasn't at all surprised to see a ring of white gold decorated with clusters of tiny diamonds surrounding an enormous sparkling sunstone. It couldn't have been more perfect. It would be a permanent reminder of the place that had brought her such happiness. Sunstone Estate.

In the Cards

By

Emily Hussey

'Do you have specific questions Rosie, or do you want a review of the year ahead?'

Rosie thought for a while. She really did want to know if new work opportunities were coming her way, but on the other hand, it would be good to have the overall picture.

'A review of the year please.'

Xaveria handed her the deck of cards. 'Concentrate on the coming year and shuffle the deck. Clear your head of mindless chatter; just focus on the year ahead.'

Rosie did as she was told, shutting her eyes to focus on positive energy and abundant thoughts. She could do with both after the miserable year that had just come to an end. She returned the deck to Xaveria and seven cards were dealt from the top, and laid out in a semi-circle.

'Interesting, very interesting,' the woman intoned.

'What do you see? Nothing bad's going to happen is it?'

'Patience young lady, patience.' Xaveria tapped the first card. 'Finance … you've been spending a bit lately and this is the year of consolidation. You need to put a proper savings plan into action.'

She must have been talking to my parents, thought Rosie. *I didn't come here for a lecture on my spending habits.*

'Health … hmm … I see an issue with your knees, or is it ankles? Do you play sport? No? Skiing perhaps? There could be a problem in the next couple of months. Work … some changes ahead. Travel … I see you taking an unexpected journey. Family … joyful news … another baby … any history of twins in your family?'

'Heavens … I don't think so. I'm not sure whether to relay that to my sister or not. She already has two little boys under three. It must be her because it certainly wouldn't be me!'

Xaveria smiled briefly and continued. 'Love … some fascinating prospects on the horizon. I see a man who has an interest in Central America. The last card indicates the highlights of the year. There could be challenges early on and you will be called upon to support others. This will bring you much satisfaction. You will move house in the second half of the year, possibly about September. Your lucky number is four, and your protective gemstone is moonstone. Keep it close to you and it will shield you from negative energies. The aura I perceive about you is orange, and this is the colour of adventure and social communication. You have an interesting year ahead.'

There was more but Rosie had forgotten most of it by the time she had paid her money and taken her leave. *Well that was a waste of time,* she thought as she made her way back up the high street. *Nothing specific about anything really. Twins—wouldn't that be a hoot, and orange—she's got to be kidding.*

Rosie by name, but not by colouring. Her hair was a deep burnished carrot, and orange was a colour she avoided like the plague. She tended to wear blues and greens as a cooling antidote to the fiery thatch. She wandered back to where she had secured her bike and unlocked the chain. It was a beautiful day, and she had opted for the bike over the car. The Saturday morning shoppers were out in force, and car parks were at a premium. Rosie felt rather smug as she zoomed along the bike lane. No parking problems for her.

Suddenly, the driver of a car parked just ahead opened a door in her path. Rosie hit the brake but with insufficient time to stop, careened into the open door. The next thing she knew, she and the bike were a tangled heap in the middle of the road as an approaching SUV bore down on her. She squeezed her eyes shut, knowing that this was it. Almost. There was a squeal of brakes and a smell of rubber. A door slammed. She felt the bike being lifted. A child was wailing in the background, or was it her?

'Are you hurt?'

She opened her eyes. Was she hurt? Yes, no, maybe. She wasn't sure of anything. A face loomed over her. It was the man who had asked the question.

'Take it easy. Can you wriggle your toes? Tell me where it hurts.'

'I'm okay. I'm fine, I think. Just a little winded. It was all so quick.'

'I'm so sorry,' the owner of the parked car babbled. 'I was distracted by the kids and didn't look before I opened the door. I'll pay if there's any damage to the bike.' The woman was distraught.

'Let's get her off the road first and we'll sort out the details later.'

It was the man again.

'Put your arm around my neck and I'll help you up.'

Rosie was aware of his strength as he hoisted her into an upright position. It was just as well he still had a firm grip on her as when she tried to take a step, a sharp pain shot through her knee, and she sagged against him.

'Right—it's a doctor for you.' He picked her up as though she were no heavier than a bag of grocery shopping and deposited her on a park bench.

'I'll secure your bike here for now and then I'll take you down to the local clinic. I'm Jared, by the way.'

For the first time, she looked at him properly. He was not conventionally handsome but there was a rugged appeal about him. She noted the aquiline nose and well-formed lips that now had a hint of a smile. One eyebrow rose slightly, as though to ask, 'Well, do I pass?' She looked away hastily. She hadn't meant to stare.

'I'm Rosie. Thanks for not running me over.'

'Well, it could have been a bit messy, and the bike might have scratched my car.'

Rosie would have laughed if her knee wasn't hurting so much. Jared secured her bike and then assisted her into the front seat of his vehicle. Once they had arrived at the clinic, he retrieved a wheelchair from inside and pushed her into the reception area.

'Look, you don't have to stay,' she said. 'I've already messed up your morning. It might be a while before the doctor sees me and I can get a taxi home after that.'

'It's no problem. I'll just make a couple of calls to re-arrange my day. I'll make myself comfy with ancient copies of *Readers' Digest* and *Golfing Australia*. Can I get you a magazine?'

In the end, they didn't have to wait long. A medical inspection decreed that nothing seemed to be broken, but that there was probably a torn ligament in the knee joint. It was strapped up, and Rosie was delivered back to the waiting room with some pain killers and instructions to rest up and apply a cold pack every 3–4 hours.

'She's not to put any stress on that knee,' the doctor advised Jared. 'You'll have to take care of her and make sure that she rests. Bring her back in three days so that I can review progress and consider whether any further treatment is required. She may need some physiotherapy to regain full mobility in that knee.'

'I'll take excellent care of her Doctor. Thank you.'

'Oh, but …'

'Now Rosie, no buts. You heard what the doctor said. Time to get you home.'

'Why did you let him think that we're a couple?' she queried as he pushed the wheelchair back to the car park. 'You don't have to take me home. I can easily get a taxi as I said before.'

'I couldn't be bothered going into explanations, and my car is much easier for you to get into than a taxi would be. You gave me such a fright today. I keep seeing you there lying in front of my wheels. For one horrible moment, I didn't think that I would be able to stop in time.'

'Nor did I actually. It wasn't your fault though so you don't have to take responsibility for me.'

'Stop quibbling and just tell me where you live. I'll drop you off, see you to your door and then I'll go. I promise.'

Rosie wondered if she should snap a photo of his car number plate with her smart phone and email it to a friend, but then felt rather silly. It wasn't as if he had done anything to make her mistrust him—quite the opposite in fact and if she was honest, she'd like to get to know him better. If she wasn't in so much pain, she would have thought about how to achieve that but right now, all she wanted to do was get home, take her pain relief and lie down for a while.

'Well, thank you. That's very kind.' She gave Jared her address and he duly delivered her to the front door. Then he took the key from her hands, unlocked the door and assisted her inside.

'Where's the kitchen? I'll get you a glass of water for those tablets and you can lie down. Is there anyone to look in on you?'

'Yes, of course. I'll give my family a call. Thank you so much Jared. I appreciate your help. I think it will be really good to lie down for a while though.'

~ * ~

Rosie didn't feel terribly rested the following day. Her mother had come over the previous evening and brought an ice pack and some soup for a light meal. It was difficult to get comfortable though and she had spent a restless night. Thoughts of the near miss when she was lying on the road kept running through her mind, and that didn't help either. She wasn't feeling her best therefore when there was a knock at the door late morning. With difficulty, she limped to answer it. Jared stood there, and her bike was leaning against the wall.

'So how are you feeling today? I put my bike rack on the car and picked up your bike for you. You left the key to the lock in my car, so I thought that I might as well bring the bike home for you. Where should I put it? I don't want to leave it there in full view of the street.'

'Umm … can you put it around the back? The side gate isn't locked. I'll open the back door for you.'

Hastily, Rosie grabbed a brush and dragged some order through her hair as she hobbled to the back door. She hadn't expected

61

a visitor and in particular not Jared. Opening the door, she saw that he had already put her bike under cover and was standing there, looking at it critically.

'It's not too bad but the front wheel has a slight buckle. You'll need to take it to a bike mechanic before you go riding again. I can recommend someone good if you don't have one. He keeps my wheels in good condition.'

'So you ride a bike too? Do come in—would you like a cup of coffee?'

'Yes I ride and yes, I'd love a cup of coffee. When you're fully mobile again, we can always do a day trip along Linear Park if you're up for it? How about you sit down and I'll make the coffee. How are you feeling?'

It was strange to see a man bustling around her kitchen. Rosie perched herself on a stool at the breakfast bar, directing Jared as to where the cups and coffee were located. He seemed quite at ease though, delivering the two steaming cups before pulling up a stool beside her.

It had given her a moment in which to observe him more closely without seeming to stare. She could see that riding his bike was probably not the only exercise he got, for he looked fit and his clothes sat comfortably on his frame. It was a nice compact derrière that sat inside his jeans. To her surprise, he was wearing a small diamond ear stud, or at least she assumed that it was diamond. Could have been synthetic but somehow he didn't seem to be a synthetic type of guy. She was intrigued enough to think that getting to know him better was something that she might enjoy.

'Before I forget, here's the key to your bike lock. It's so tiny; it's easy to overlook it.'

'Don't I know it. I'm forever misplacing it. Thanks for bringing the bike back. To be honest, I'd totally forgotten about it. I'm a bit tied to the house for now anyway so I couldn't have picked it up.'

'Do you need to go anywhere?'

'No ... lucky that it's a Sunday. My mother's picking up some crutches for me from the clinic and I've arranged a lift to work tomorrow so I'll be fine through the week. For today though, I'm stuck here and I'm happy just to take it easy.'

'Well the doctor did say to rest up and keep off your feet. Look, I don't want to intrude on you now; you probably need to relax this afternoon, but what about if I come back this evening with some takeaway?'

'Jared, you've done enough for me already. I don't expect you to feed me as well.'

'I don't really see you hobbling around the kitchen this evening, crutches or not. I can see by your face that you should be lying down again. How about we relocate to the living room and you can lie down on your couch.'

Jared carried their coffees and Rosie manoeuvred herself to the living room. It was a relief to lie down again. Jared made sure that the television remote was in easy reach and that she had a couple of books nearby. Rosie had a stack of library books sitting on a shelf and for a while they discussed reading preferences, before Jared said that he should leave her to it.

'I might just snooze for a while,' Rosie said. 'I didn't sleep so well last night so a nanna nap would be good.'

With arrangements made about the time he would return, and her food preferences noted, Jared departed leaving Rosie to her thoughts. Scattered thoughts they were too. She was half bemused at the turn of events that had introduced her to Jared and half unsure of where things might be heading. On top of that, where did she want them to head? Too many questions. She snoozed instead.

By the time Jared returned, Rosie had showered and changed and was learning to manoeuvre her way around the house with the crutches that her mother had delivered. It was slow progress, but she had managed to put some wine in the fridge to chill, and set the table. He arrived exactly when he said he would.

'Well you've got a bit more colour in your cheeks now. Your nap must have done you good. Show me the plates and I'll sort this food out.'

'I can do that,' Rosie protested. 'It's just my knee that's the problem. The rest of me's fine.'

'I've noticed,' he said, giving her a glance that was imbued with meaning. 'The rest of you is *more* than fine. No point in undoing the good work you've done today though. Sit down and I'll bring it all over. I can see that the table is ready so you've done your bit.'

Rosie had to satisfy her need to be hospitable by getting the wine from the fridge, and pouring them each a glass. The meal was relaxed, with each supplying information about their work, their families and interests in general. It was the sort of detail which was part of the *getting-to-know-you* ritual, but there hadn't been time previously. They had both done a bit of travelling and hoped to do some more; both had learnt rudimentary Italian, and both enjoyed cooking. Flavour of the month for Jared was Mexican but Rosie was experimenting with Vietnamese.

'I nearly forgot,' he exclaimed when the meal was finished but they were still finishing their wine. 'I brought you something—sorry, it's not gift-wrapped.'

From his pocket, he took a small paper bag. Rosie recognised the logo as being from the gift shop that was adjacent to where they had left her bike the day before.

'I love surprises Jared, but I wasn't expecting a gift. You even brought the meal.'

'I know, but I thought this would be useful. Have a look.'

Opening the bag, Rosie drew out a key ring. It was decorated with a small orange cabochon set in silver. As she examined it, taken with the unusual colouring, the stone reacted with flashes of reflected light.

'It's for that little bike key so that you don't have any problems finding it in the future. It's set with a sunstone.'

'It's beautiful—thank you.' Impulsively, Rosie reached across the table to touch his hand. 'I can't thank you enough for all the help you've been.'

His eyes met hers across the table, and his smile held the promise of good times to come. Rosie was aware of the butterflies that were starting to dance the fandango in the pit of her stomach.

It was only after he had gone, much later, with the promise made of their next meeting that Rosie was able to reflect on the weekend. Xaveria had been right after all—well nearly right. She did have a problem with her knee, there were interesting prospects on the horizon, and it did look like being an interesting year ahead. She had just been confused about the stone; it should have been sunstone, not moonstone and as for twins—no way!

ROMANCE
WRITERS
of Australia

An Enticing Proposition

By

Jillian Jones

Jane watched as Doug worked the room. He was rude and pompous when instructing the wait staff, yet sickeningly charming to the socialites that he was sucking up to. It suddenly occurred to her that he was also being just as two-faced in their relationship. She gratefully swapped her empty champagne flute for a full one from a passing waiter.

'He's not your type,' said the waiter.

'Excuse me?' Jane replied as she looked up and smiled seeing it was Xavier, her favourite kitchen hand at the hospital. No doubt he was recruited because they were short staffed tonight. Doug kept a lean team.

'He's conceited, don't waste your time with him,' he continued, in his beautiful British accent.

'Xavier! He's your boss! You might want to keep your opinions to yourself if you want to keep your job.'

'Okay, but beware, I've noticed you've been watching him for most of the evening.' Xavier ran his long slender fingers through his honey-blond hair as if he was pushing his hair back into place, but there was never a hair out of place on Xavier's head. Jane had for some time realised this was a quirky habit of his when he was feeling a little unsure of himself.

'I have not,' she said, taking a big sip of champagne.

'Do you know he's married? Plus he's the most self-centred person I know, oh, there's his wife now.'

Xavier continued on his rounds while Jane watched in horror as an attractive and very heavily pregnant blonde sauntered up to Doug's side and slid her hand in his. Doug seemed very happy to introduce her to the patron he'd been fawning all over. It was time to send the text.

Jane walked out to the balcony to get some fresh air and avoid any eye contact with Doug once he'd had the chance to read her text. She felt like a weight had been lifted from her shoulders. Xavier's arrival at the hospital had changed things. The past three weeks had been wonderful. They'd gone for drinks each Friday night with six other staff members and then each Saturday, Xavier had something arranged. They'd hiked, kayaked, been to the cinemas, visited a theme park and dined out, just the two of them. Not that he'd offered her anything other than friendship but she savoured every moment of the time she'd spent in his company.

'Oh there you are.' It was Xavier again. 'Oh, no. The sun has gone from your sunstones. What's troubling you?' There was genuine concern on his face. Jane smiled. That was the other thing about Xavier. The moment he met her, he insisted Jane's eyes were mesmerising and that they held a ring of sunstone within them. Jane couldn't see what he was talking about. Her eyes were hazel; predominantly a greenish colour but there was a small ring of blue at the edge of her iris and a ring of light brown just around her pupil. However, Xavier had continued for the past three weeks with the sunstone story and insisted he could read her mood by the intensity of colour in her ring of sunstone. Whatever.

'I just needed some fresh air,' she replied.

'Well, I'm finished now and I'm heading to a nightclub with the rest of the Friday night gang. Are you going to join us?'

'I'd love to,' she said.

~ * ~

68

Jane settled herself back on her bar stool and handed out the drinks.

'So, Jane?' said John, the head cook from the maternity ward, as she handed him a gin and tonic.

'We're sharing the sordid details of our pathetic sex lives and it seems none of us are getting any. Can you add a bit of excitement to the conversation?' he said, with a wry smile.

Jane hid her surprise and embarrassment well.

'Sorry John. There's nothing exciting happening in my bedroom, or anywhere else in my apartment for that matter,' she said with a dramatic pout, followed by a laugh as she passed a beer to Xavier, avoiding eye contact with him. She took a sip of her wine and listened to the laughter peel around the table.

'Oh well Xav, lucky last, you're a good-looking guy, you have to be getting lucky?'

'Not for a very long time, that's why I thought I'd venture to Australia. I heard the girls were more willing, but so far I've been here a month with no luck.' He laughed as he took a sip of his beer.

'Well, you pathetic bunch, I'm off to change all that,' John announced as he slid off his seat.

'Good luck my friend,' said Xavier. 'Me? I'd like to hit the dance floor. Would anyone care to join me?'

Jane, and Helen from cardiology, said yes but Helen only lasted two songs. Jane wasn't keen to leave the floor. Xavier was too much fun and such a great dancer but after the fourth song, a slow dance number filled the speakers and Jane turned to leave. Xavier took her hand and playfully pulled her in close. Jane used all her willpower to slow her breath and palpitating heart. His closeness, his cologne and his eyes were overwhelming her. She'd fallen for him the moment they were introduced on his first day at the hospital, but so had numerous other staff members, male and female. And she'd had nothing but *just friends* vibes from him. She didn't want to lose his friendship but she also didn't want to let go of a moment that held so much possibility.

'I told a lie back there,' she whispered in his ear.

'What do you mean?' he looked confused.

'I've been having an affair with Doug. I only stopped when I met you.' Tears welled in her eyes. 'When we first got together he told me his marriage was over and he was just looking for the right moment to leave his wife but I was okay with his proposition of sex on Saturday morning with no strings attached. I thought I was happy on my own. I thought I didn't need more of a commitment but the time I've spent with you these past three weeks has made me realise I want more. I've avoided the Saturday morning rendezvous with Doug because I don't want just sex anymore and tonight I sent him a text calling it off.' She caught a tear as it rolled down her cheek.

'How long has it been going on? Does anyone else know?' Xavier asked, calmly.

'Two years and no, I've told no one, not even my family or closest friends.' The surprised expression on his face made her feel uncomfortable. Jane looked down. She felt incapable of giving him a rational explanation for her choices to stay in the arrangement and to not tell anyone about it. It just was. And she hadn't gone searching for a better alternative.

'Wow, I'm so sorry.' Xavier lifted her chin so her eyes met his for a moment.

'Jane, you deserve better.' He brushed his thumb over her lips, sending a shiver of pleasure through her, and kissed her gently. 'You deserve someone that knows how to make your eyes shine like the sun,' he whispered. Then he held her close for the rest of the song. Her head resting on his shoulder, the feeling of his body against hers escalated her longing.

'Take me home Xavier, I don't mind if it's yours or mine,' she said, pulling slightly from his hold so she could look into his eyes.

'I thought you'd never ask,' he smiled. 'Mine's closer.'

~ * ~

Jane sat and marvelled at the majestic view of the river from Xavier's apartment. She'd been too distracted to notice it when he invited her in last night. But now that they were finally out of bed and Xavier was making a coffee, she had a chance to look around.

'Xavier, don't take this the wrong way but how can a kitchen hand afford this place?'

Xavier walked around the kitchen bench and handed her a coffee. 'Jane, there's something I need to tell you.'

'What's that?'

'I'm a Prince.'

'What? Are you in a play at the hospital or something?' She searched his azure blue eyes for a deeper understanding of his words.

'No, I'm really a Prince,' he sighed. 'I know, right? You don't hear that every day,' he cringed, possibly having noticed the blank look on her face. 'I'm the heir to the throne of a principality in Europe. I'm here just taking some time out.'

'Is this a joke?' She scowled. 'Because it's not funny.' Tears of confusion welled in her eyes.

'No, and I should have told you sooner. I was just playing it safe. I didn't want my true identity getting in the way of our relationship. I'm still the same person. Everything I've told you about myself, and my family is the truth. I just left out a few extra details about my work, my surname and exactly where I live in Europe and the royalty bit,' he said apologetically.

'So where does that leave us?' she asked, after a long pause that involved staring into her coffee cup, somehow hoping it would help her absorb the information.

Xavier sat down beside her, brushed her cheek gently and lovingly then lifted her chin so her eyes meet his.

'It makes me feel so sad to see how pale the sunstone is in your eyes. What can I do to bring back their sparkle?' He sighed, and then kissed her lips tenderly. She savoured the taste and returned his kiss with increasing passion. He was hard to resist and her question remained unanswered, much to her relief. Jane was sure Xavier's answer wouldn't be what she wanted to hear when he did finally tell her. So she resolved within her heart and mind to treasure every moment she had with him. She had no intention of raising the question again.

~ * ~

On Monday afternoon, Jane waved encouragingly to the children as they left the art room to return to their wards. It touched her soul to see how they forgot their dire health conditions for a brief moment as they lost themselves in their creativity. Suddenly she noticed Xavier at the door.

'Hello,' she said cheerfully. He was such a shining light in this heavy environment as he walked in to collect the food trays.

'Hi Jane, nice to see the children being inspired in your capable hands.' He smiled and kissed her cheek.

'Thanks,' she replied shyly, still finding his compliments hard to receive. 'But, I'm not the inspiring one, they are.'

'You're too humble,' he replied. He paused and looked around to make sure they were alone. 'And I've just heard from Doug that he and you are a couple.'

'What?' She was stunned.

'Well, I think he only told me to put me in my place. He said he intends to put a stop to our relationship and has organised for my transfer to another hospital but only because he can't fire me as a result of my connection to the Chair of the hospital board.'

Jane felt a flood of disappointment at the thought of not seeing Xavier each day. Xavier was clearly annoyed but nothing further could be said as the Warden arrived to see how the art class went.

~ * ~

A week later, Jane felt light and joyful as she danced around the circle of stones. She rang the small bells that were wrapped around her fingers with brightly coloured ribbons. She felt her ponytail swing from side to side in response to the rhythm of her body. In the light of the setting sun, the beach looked like paradise. She circled around the stones once more, deliberately making the full skirt of her navy blue maxi dress swirl in and out like an ocean wave, much to the thrill of the small girls dancing along beside her. She laughed at their excitement, slowed down, stopped and handed the bells back to the girl who had insisted she dance with them.

Xavier's smile made her knees go weak as he offered her his hand so they could continue their walk along the beach. And her heart skipped a beat as their hands connected. She drank in his mesmerisingly toned biceps. She longed to run her hand over them, along his bare, muscular chest and down his six-pack abs. But that would have to wait. They had all week because Xavier had booked a beach holiday thinking it would be nice to spend some time together before he started his new job.

'That was fun, you should have had a go.' She smiled and turned and waved goodbye to the excited group of children enjoying the warm and sunny afternoon at the resort.

'I had more fun watching you.' His hand was warm and tantalising in hers. She stood on tiptoes and gave him a playful kiss on the lips as they walked. He was just the perfect height. Something she appreciated given she was tall for a woman.

'Jane, I came to Australia for two reasons. It was my intention to meet a down-to-earth girl who would make a good wife. I wanted to meet someone who was genuinely interested in me and not my position. I believe I've successfully achieved that so now I want to travel around Australia and I would like you to join me. Then, I want you to come to Europe with me,' he said. Jane detected a note of nervousness in his voice. She glanced up to see him run his fingers through his hair, his gaze directed at his feet. She walked along silently attempting to process what he'd just said. She couldn't help thinking how nonchalantly he'd presented the proposition.

'I love how you are with children. I love how discreet you were in your relationship with Doug and in situations around the children at the hospital. I love your creativity, positivity and your passion for life.' He paused, stopped and turned to look at her. 'I just love everything about you. And, I'm selfish. I want our hospital and our community centres back home to benefit from your energy,' he took in a deep breath. 'Will you at least think about coming to Europe with me and give some consideration to the idea of marrying me? I know becoming my wife won't be an easy path but I believe we can work through it.'

She looked into his eyes and felt the intensity of his penetrating gaze as he waited for her to respond. It was only a month since she'd met him but she knew he was the one. She trusted Xavier. He was the most communicative and emotionally open and honest man she'd ever met. She'd never been this happy in a relationship before.

'I know from your eyes that's a yes,' he smiled. 'The ring of sunstone in them is sparkling brighter than I've ever seen it.' She rolled her eyes.

'Well, that's the most enticing proposition I've ever had, Xavier. And, yes, I'm willing if you are,' she smiled. 'So where exactly is this principality of yours?'

Say the Words

By

Emmeline Lock

If she stood watching long enough, Maggie McArthur could see the dog move. But it only moved its gold and white head and only from side to side.

It watched a man swim, cutting efficiently through the water between the yacht club and the fisherman's wharf. Up and back, up and back.

At the counter of her Beachwalk Cafe, where she prepped for the day ahead, she knew that she could look out every summer's day, come screaming northerlies or sideways rain, and the dog would be there.

She had to break some occupational safety rules to see the man in the water, though. The way to do it was to put a step stool onto an upturned empty tub and peer out of the high, long window above the espresso machine. Her personal rule was that she was only allowed to climb up after she'd sliced the truss tomatoes, turned the donut oil to heat and arranged the cheese slices into the refrigerated cabinet, ready for the Sunday lunch crowd.

Then, she'd spend some quality time … critiquing his stroke. He moved economically, his large hands slicing through the water, water sluicing down his muscled back.

If he ever found out that she spent a sizeable chunk of each morning ogling him out her high window and had done since he'd come to town a month before, he might rethink his fitness routine and buy himself a treadmill.

Today, he finished his swim before she realised it was seven-thirty. He whistled up the dog as he strode with long, tanned legs from the water, his sandy hair flipping in all directions. He shoved a hand through it to stop the water dripping into his eyes.

Heart bumping up against her collarbones, Maggie leaped from her high perch and raced to the door. She unlocked it, flipped the sign to OPEN, leaped back behind the counter and then aligned the pens with the order booklet until she heard the soft sounds of a towel vigorously rubbed over a body and a quiet command for the dog.

'Stay, Banjo.' Towel slung around his neck, the man opened the screen door and closed it behind him, not a drop of water falling to mar the floor she'd cleaned last night.

'Morning, Maggie.' She wondered if he'd ever been a toothpaste model. He should totally model dental hygiene tools. If Maggie were a dentist, she'd recommend him. She was pretty sure the next nine female dentists she asked would say the same.

'Hi, Will. How's the water today?' Maggie winced internally. She asked that every morning. Mental note: find a new opening line. She hoped he wouldn't remember that she'd asked that yesterday.

The corner of his mouth lifted. He remembered. 'It was good, thanks. Wet and salty.' His eyes narrowed slightly. The same thing he said every time, too.

'The usual for you today? Large flat white and a regular frothed milk?'

'Thanks, that'd be great.'

Maggie got the full cream milk out on her way to the espresso machine, then stood grinding coffee, flicking buttons and turning taps.

Will moved up the counter a few steps so he was even with her, watching her as she worked.

'It looks complicated, that machine. How many years of university do you need to do to use that?'

She huffed out a laugh. 'Not a one. You can knock off the training in half a day. It's not rocket science.'

'I've had some coffee that has tasted a lot like the fuel NASA might use. Yours is far superior to that.'

'I bet half the kids in the senior year at school already know how to make coffee.'

'Well, they do have an excellent principal.' Will made a half fist, blew on his fingernails, then buffed them on his damp towel, wiggling his eyebrows.

Maggie grinned and waved her free hand at the drinks prep area. 'In fact, Minnie Nelson helps out here on the weekends during peak times. Girl makes a killer latte.'

He rubbed his chin with a large, tanned hand. Maggie heard stubble rasping and the small hairs at her hairline stood up. He was new to the school this year, she recalled, he probably wouldn't know Minnie. Even though she currently had hair coloured like a tropical sea.

'Ah, Minnie.' Will clicked his fingers. 'Good debater.'

Maggie slanted him a look. Yes, that was Minnie.

'Of course, it's hard to forget the blue hair too,' he chuckled.

Maggie laughed, topping off his flat white and capping both the drinks. 'She's one of a kind. A talented crafter, too. She makes these sunstone key rings that I sell on consignment. I move about thirty a week.' Maggie indicated to the rotating wire stand adjacent to the register, where the flat local shells hung from their silver loops. She pushed the drinks forward. 'Pop these on your account?'

'Thanks, if you would.' He patted the thigh of his damp swimming shorts, the wet fabric slapping against his skin. 'Not much room in here for a wallet.'

Now she was thinking about the inside of his shorts. 'Thanks for stopping by.'

He reached for the drinks just as she did and the combined force of their hands popped the lid off the smaller cup. It spun off to the right, skidding across the counter. They both lurched to grab it, their upper arms crashing together.

Maggie ended up with a handful of lid. Will ended up with a fistful of Maggie's hair.

They both straightened, but he didn't let go her braid.

Instead, he rubbed the strands beneath the band between his fingers, his eyes on hers.

'It's soft,' he murmured.

Maggie watched her black curls wind around his long fingers. She swallowed and laughed nervously.

'You should see it when it's loose and I'm down on the back beach. It deserves its own special ring of hell, then.'

His eyes met hers and she lost herself for a moment. They were grey, like the sea under summer storm clouds.

'I'd like to see that,' he said quietly.

'I should cut it off. It's not the best beach hair.'

He searched her face. 'That would be a shame, I think.'

The chime on the door clanged and a gravelly voice rang out.

'Maggie my love, I need some hot donuts. Due at the doctor in fifteen, and he's surely going to make me give them up, so I'd better get—oh, I do apologise.'

Mr Wyght blustered into the small shop. What he lacked in hearing, he made up for in charm.

Will laughed quietly and gave Maggie's braid a gentle tug. 'I'll see you tomorrow morning.'

Maggie smiled back at him before turning to Mr Wyght, the feeling that something momentous had just happened echoing around in her. 'Will that be six or a dozen, Mr W?'

'Just the two, Miss Maggie. Martha's got me on one of those diet things.'

She heard Banjo whuff a quiet greeting from outside as she picked up the silver donut squeezer, then watched Will jog carefully across the paved waterfront to a white dual-cab ute. He whistled Banjo to get up, holding up the paper cup of milk for the animal to drink from while he sipped his coffee with his free hand.

Maggie turned to the donut prep area, automatically searching by the register for the black marker she used to write the customer name on the donut bag. Not finding it, she opened a nearby drawer, got out a second one and used it to write 'Mr W' on the bag. She added a caricature of a dolphin wearing sunglasses.

She sugared the donuts, bagged them and smiled as Mr Wyght exclaimed over the picture on his bag. By the time the screen door closed on him, on his way with a napkin to use before he saw the doctor, the bronzed man and his golden dog were gone.

~ * ~

Maggie's knife flew as she prepped her tomatoes before she assumed her morning position peering out the high window. She checked out the main window. Yes, Danjo was on the beach, watching.

Toes curling over the edge of the step stool, she could see Will, his body moving smoothly through the waves, his freestyle stroke loose and effortless.

A pale shape in the corner of her vision made her stop. In the far corner of the outside sill was a sunstone, featuring the ragged gold circle at the centre of the cream-coloured disk that gave the shell its name. It wasn't a real gemstone, not like the sunstone that had been discovered overseas, but an enterprising local had called the worn, discarded home of some sea creature a sunstone years before and it had stuck.

She shuffled her feet to the right edge of the footstool and slid the window open with the tips of her three longest fingers. With a frown, she pulled the sunstone inside and looked at it. In the middle of the shell was a black question mark.

Weird. Maybe a seagull had put it there, though they were more interested in taking your hot chips and the last mouthful of your ice-cream cone from your fingers than in shells.

Shrugging, Maggie tucked the stone into the palm of her hand and slid the window shut.

Looking out at the ocean, she let out a little squeak. Will wasn't in the water any more. It must be half past. Launching herself off her rickety platform, she flew around the counter and unlocked the door.

When she turned the OPEN sign, she saw Will's face. He grinned and waved. Maggie swore she could *hear* the blood rushing through her veins to her face.

She opened the door and stepped back for him to enter. 'Morning, Maggie.'

'Hi Will, how's the water today?' Oh, God. She was meant to remember not to say that. She slunk behind the counter.

'It was good, thanks. Wet and salty.' Will squeezed the thin part high on his nose briefly, then laughed as he shook his head. 'I'll have the usual, thanks Maggie.'

'No worries.' As she rang it up, the sunstone she had clutched in her hand fell to the counter, spinning and rattling before it settled. She slapped a hand over it and slid it next to the order book before moving to the espresso machine.

With her back to him, she only heard the slide and click as he picked up the stone. 'Been treasure hunting?'

She looked over her shoulder at him and shook her head. 'I do collect them on the back beach in the evenings, but no, I found that one … elsewhere.'

'A question mark,' he said. 'Is it supposed to mean something? A message, maybe?'

Maggie raised her voice to be heard over the frother. 'It was in a kind of difficult place to get to. I'm not sure I would have found it if I hadn't been, ah, getting something from high up. Probably some animal left it behind.'

'It's a bit odd, but you're probably right.'

She lidded both the finished drinks.

When she turned, he was looking at her, no smile on his face. It didn't last long, though and his lips tipped up.

She smiled back. 'I'll put it on the account. Have a great day, Will.'

'I will, thanks. I'll … see you around, Maggie.' He seemed like he wanted to say more but he stepped back as Mr Wyght blustered through the door, yelling out before it was shut, 'Good news, Maggie my darling! The doc says I'm allowed the donuts, so long as I don't overdo it. So, I'll just have the four today. I'm celebrating!'

'Happy days, Mr Wyght. Coming right up.' Maggie waved to Will as he sidestepped Mr W with a nod and left with the beverages for himself and his dog.

~ * ~

By Friday evening, Will had been into the shop six times and she'd sold eighty per cent of the sunstone key rings. Mr Wyght had consumed twenty donuts, after the two extras on Tuesday and two more extras on Friday afternoon after a run-in with his wife, who had told him if he ate many more donuts, he'd start looking like one.

She also had five sunstones, the next four having a single word on them.

Late Tuesday, she'd found the second one resting in the base of the uppermost cup in the regular takeaway stack. Another had been in the register on the account book and one had been under the stand of sunstone key rings. The final one had been inside of Mr Wyght's donut bag, making her picture of a smiling cartoon sun a bit bumpy.

This morning, she'd taken out her new black marker and written some words of her own.

The five word stones rested in the side pocket of her dress as she walked on the back beach searching for new sunstones for Minnie to work on.

She pressed a hand to her stomach. Had her words even been read?

Stopping, she forced her shoulders down and looked out over the ocean. It was gorgeously flat, the hot north wind that had been blowing sand against the legs of beachgoers this morning had dropped, leaving a warm, pink stillness behind. It was unusual to be down on the beach without her hair flying into her mouth and she gathered it behind her head then laid it over her shoulder. It was nice to be out of that braid.

A wet nose in her palm made her jump. She knelt to the soggy, gritty dog, who dropped the tennis ball he'd been carrying and it rolled to a stop against her foot.

'Oh hey, Banjo.' She scruffed him around the ears. 'How's the water today?'

'Wet and salty.'

Maggie rose to see Will approaching from the walkway behind the caravan park. The ball rolled away from Maggie's foot towards the water and Banjo loped after it, barking at seagulls as he went, tongue lolling.

'Well that's what I'd say, even if I had every intention of saying something different for once.'

Maggie drank in the sight of Will. He was wearing a soft grey T-shirt, unlike his morning uniform, but she had to appreciate how he filled it out and the way the well-loved jean shorts stretched over his thigh muscles.

'Hey, Will.'

'Hey, Maggie. You look lovely.'

Smoothing her hands over the dress, she shot him a smile. 'Bit different to the work uniform.'

'I'll say.' He watched her hands as they moved along her sides, then he swallowed and stepped toward her. 'How was your week?'

Sand crunched under her bare feet as she moved close enough to feel his body heat through the thin fabric, close enough to maybe reach out and touch him.

'It was good. Busy.' She delved into her pocket. 'It was also a bit strange. I kept finding these written-on sunstones throughout my shop.'

She held her palm out flat between his body and hers, the stones in a jumble.

'Did you?' Will reached out and moved the stones on her outstretched hand, so the words faced her and formed a sentence, his fingertips warm against her skin.

'I nearly fed one to Mr Wyght.'

He choked, then coughed.

She laughed. 'It was fine, I've handled enough of those bags to know when one feels a little heavy.'

'Well, that's a relief. Imagine what his doctor would have to say about his diet then.'

Maggie laughed, but it leaked out of her, powerless, when she saw that Will had finished arranging the stones in her hand.

May

I
kiss
you
?

'I've been wanting to see this loose.' Will reached forward and slid his hand through the hair that lay over her shoulder. 'It's beautiful. I like how it curls around my fingers.'

He blinked and looked at her. 'It's funny, you know. I received a few words myself this morning.' He used her hair to gently pull her closer and she followed the tug, until their bare toes were touching in the sand.

'Did you really?'

'Well, *I* didn't, truth be told. Banjo did. But I assumed the message was for me, because while he's got lots of potential girlfriends, none of them can write.'

Maggie laughed, but didn't move her gaze from his face, the tawny skin around his eyes creasing as he grinned at her.

Reaching into his pocket with his free hand, he retrieved a white plastic lid from a regular takeaway coffee cup and a black marker pen. He waved the marker at her before he tucked it back into his pocket. He settled his hand, palm up, touching hers. On it, he placed the lid upside down so that the words were visible and facing him.

Yes.
Please.

'I'll let you get back to collecting your sunstones shortly, because I have a few more words I'd like to write to you.' He slid his free hand through her hair, the mass falling over his arm, the gentle pull sending pulses of deliciousness through her.

'Take your time,' Maggie murmured before their lips met. 'We've got all summer.'

His mouth, soft and warm, moved over hers. She felt him, felt his kiss, at the end of every nerve, in every cell of her body, in her blood. The items in their hands fell to the sand, to be collected later. She sucked gently on his bottom lip and he hissed in a breath, his hands moving to her waist where he held her pressed to his hard body.

He lifted his head slowly, the grey of his eyes intense and stormy. There was no laughter in them now. Far distant, Banjo barked at more birds. 'What if I want longer?'

She wound her fingers through his hair and pulled him closer. 'I've got more sunstones. Just say the words.'

The Sunstone Bride

By

Fiona Marsden

Cassia huddled in the depths of the undercroft, hardly daring to breath. Luca burrowed his small frame under her cloak, smothering a whimper against her breasts. The others had fled to the forest at first warning, not noticing one child absent from the nursery. The appearance of the boy in the window of the solar had drawn her back from safety. Now the chance to escape was lost.

The heavy thud of more than one set of booted feet sounded on the timber stairs. 'The household has fled, Eiric. We can resupply and continue the search.'

He spoke in the common tongue, thick and guttural. Like the raiders from the northeast. Peering through the gap in the barrels, she could see him. A big man with a lined face, in faded blue tunic and rabbit fur vest. The other, she could see only a portion of his broad shoulders and straw-coloured hair, braided down his back with leather strips. A tall man, well made.

'We'll take only what we need. Fetch the lads down to collect it. The doors over there can be opened and the horses loaded in the courtyard. We need to be well away by sunset.'

The other man left with a muttered acknowledgement, leaving the larger man alone. Cassia drew back as piercing blue eyes delved into the shadows. Luca gasped and clung tightly. Full on, the raider was a fearsome sight, his bearded face marred by a thick ridge of scar tissue down one cheek and lifting the end of his mouth in a permanent sneer.

He must have heard Luca for he approached the barrels, drawing his sword in a swift movement. 'Who hides from Eiric Skeller?'

Eiric the Twisted? Cassia rose to her feet, holding tightly to Luca. 'Spare the boy. He's done no harm.'

The sword dropped a fraction as he stood back to allow her to skirt the barrels and face him. 'So the lad has done no harm? What of you? What offence do you have on your conscience?'

'Nought, sir. I only ask you let the boy go. He's barely five summers old. No threat to you or your men.'

The eyes glinted in the late morning light from the unshuttered windows. 'He's not much of anything at that size. You, on the other hand, have something about you of purpose.'

'I'm not important. They won't ransom me, if you think to make a profit.'

His gaze skimmed over her. He would see the patches on both cloak and surcoat. 'A servant?'

'No. I am a relative of no account.'

The twist of his lips suggested humour, but his hand gripped the sword firmly. 'A dowerless female. A sad addition to an otherwise prosperous holding.'

'I am of use, master raider. I earn my keep unlike those who steal the produce of other men's toil.'

'A sharp tongue also. No wonder you are unwed at such an advanced age.'

'Two and twenty is not so old. What makes you think me unwed?'

'Were you mine, I'd not be content to leave you to the hands of marauders such as ourselves.' The sword lifted the edge of the cloak from where she held the boy. 'No ring to bind you. I think we know your position.'

He was right. None would care what happened to her. Only the loss of a pair of hands when it came to caring for the children, or working in the kitchens. The sword slid back into the sheath. 'What will you do with us?'

'Show me around. The boy can come too so he can stay under your eye.'

An hour later, Luca had wilted. The raider was thorough, delving into every storeroom, every nook and cranny. The older man came too, making marks on a stick of wood with a small knife as they counted bags of flour and meal, separated out roots and herbs to be taken. 'Why do you divide them up?'

'We are coming into autumn. Would you have us leave you with nothing to eat through the winter?'

'What do you care? Raiders take what they want and leave carnage behind.'

'Is this what you expect? That we will empty your stores and throw a faggot on the remains as we leave?'

Cassia kept her voice steady. 'From all I hear, yes.'

'You are either brave or foolish. I have not decided which.' His fingers gripped her jaw, turning her face up so she was forced to look at him.

'It would be foolish to expect mercy from the likes of you.'

The fingers squeezed until her skin must purple from the pressure. 'You judge us harshly. What cause do you have to think us barbarians?'

'You have a hasty temper, master raider. I think you would sooner hurt than heal.'

He flung her away from him with a low growl. 'Put the boy to bed before he drops where he stands. You may stay with him to ensure his safety from my men.'

The sarcasm in his tone bit deeply. He had been considerate, both of her and the boy, keeping them close and warding off the lascivious stares of some of his men. They must respect him, for they kept their distance. 'Are you leaving?'

'Not yet. Will you miss me?'

His laughter followed her up the stairs to the solar. She kept herself stiff and straight until she was out of his sight. Luca could sleep on the carpet with a soft blanket while she watched from the windows. She was anxious for them to leave. Could not wait to see the last of that mocking face, that … that raider.

~ * ~

The girl was a little undersized, but womanly in shape. It was good she was out of his sight for a time so he could focus on outfitting his men for the next stage of the journey. They had ventured further south than planned. From here they must strike north before heading west again. His runaway bride and her lover had made good time in their escape. They would be aiming for Wales and from there, across the water to Dublin. He had vowed to follow them to the ends of the earth if he must.

He strode out to the courtyard. The horses looked to be refreshed. His men knew their jobs, packing the food and supplies into easily carried loads for the packhorses. A sensation of being watched drew his gaze to the windows of the solar, overhanging the courtyard. He hadn't asked her name. Not that it mattered. Tomorrow she would be a memory. A faint recollection of wide eyes the colour of peat and soft brown hair glimpsed under the loosened wimple.

Raising a hand, he grinned up at her frowning face. He caught the flash of a pale hand quickly withdrawn as she stepped back from the window. *Stubborn wench.*

A signal from one of the men on guard duty took him to the gateway. 'They are watching, M'Lord.'

'Are they gathering arms?'

'It doesn't appear so. Seems to be observing more than any other activity.'

'Good. We're nearly ready. The boy can be sent across the field by himself.'

'What of the woman?'

Eiric looked up at the windows. She might not be visible, but she was watching. 'I'll take her with us. A bond for good behaviour.'

'We don't have a spare horse.'

'She's small enough to ride pillion without slowing us down. My Thundercloud is strong enough for two.'

He went back to the men preparing the horses to give them instructions. 'A pad for a lady to ride behind me. Use something from the croft. They seem well supplied with woollen blankets.' And now for the woman.

~ * ~

He was coming to bid farewell. What else would he want with her?

Luca pushed away the bowl of soup she'd brought from the kitchens once he was awake and hungry. 'What will happen now?'

'They are leaving.' The joy she should feel was somehow absent. It had nothing to do with the raider. It must be the distress her cousin and his family would be feeling over the loss of supplies to get them through the coming winter.

'Pack your things.'

His order grated against her ears. 'Why? What purpose will it serve?'

'I need a hostage. To ensure we aren't followed.'

Her heart leapt to her throat. 'You have no need of a hostage. My kin are farmers, not warriors.'

'Would you hazard a guess a lad isn't running hotfoot to your lord's keep to sound an alarm?'

She stayed silent, knowing he was right. Roland would want to ensure he stayed in the good graces of his overlord. An early report of raiders crossing his lands would bring a reward.

'We don't have time to waste. Pack your belongings. Only what you need for a journey of a week or two.'

'A week or two? Where are you taking me?'

He looked at Luca and shook his head. 'I'll not tell you now. You will be returned safely when we are far enough away to ensure there is no pursuit.'

Still she hesitated. It seemed strange to take a hostage to prevent pursuit.

He shrugged those wide shoulders and patted the downy head of the boy. 'I could take the boy, but it will be hard travelling for a child.'

Heat rose in her chest. 'Barbarian.' She dragged the boy away from the large, strangely gentle hand. 'I will join you. If you insist.'

With an annoying smirk, he turned away. 'We await your presence, M'Lady.'

Pig. But that were to insult the pigs.

In the room she shared with her cousin's elder daughters, Cassia shoved her meagre belongings into a sack. Under Luca's interested gaze, she picked up the small carved box that held all the wealth her parents left behind. Nothing of real value. A string of amber beads of her mother's and a battered shield brooch of bronze set with a rough-polished yellow stone. After a moment of hesitation, she pushed it deep into the sack so her clothes concealed the shape.

He hardly noticed when she made her appearance in the courtyard, busy giving orders in his own language. The older man took the sack and tied it to a horse carrying a wooden chest. There were a score of horses in all, four of them laden only with goods, the others with riders. As well as swords, some carried hunting bows. Most wore leather jerkins over their tunics and fur-lined capes were strapped behind the saddles.

All but the big dappled grey. His empty saddle was richly carved and behind it, a padded cushion for a pillion. Before she could protest, large hands lifted her onto the broad rump of the beast. The horse shifted uneasily but stilled at a word and soft caress from his master. She gripped the high back of the saddle, snatching her fingers back as the raider mounted, settling his large body far too close for comfort. 'Hold on.'

She did as commanded, wrapping her arms around his middle. 'What is happening with Luca?'

'We'll drop him in the field as we go, in reach of his mother. They are on the watch.'

The cortège left the holding, striking out across the fallow fields toward the forest. They stopped out of reach of arrow shot and the boy was placed on the ground. To her surprise, a small purse that jingled as if with coin was placed in the boy's hand by the older man. 'Run boy. Your mother awaits.'

Luca paused only for a last glance at Cassia before breaking into a run. A woman's voice came from the forests edge and several figures appeared.

A sharp command and the horsemen broke into a gallop. Tightening her grip, Cassia took a last look at her kinfolk. She doubted she would see them again.

Hours later, the sun long set, they stopped in a clearing with the intention of camping. Cassia was lifted from the horse by the older man. He steadied her while Eiric dismounted and issued orders. Every bone ached and her fingers were numb from holding on.

She almost fell into the raider's arms when the other man went to deal with the horses.

'A hard journey. I'm sorry for it but we have no time to waste.'

He pulled her gloves from her hands and rubbed them vigorously. Her spirit revived a little under the rough handling. 'Perhaps a different calling would mean less trouble.'

'We are not fleeing. We are pursuing.'

'With so many men?'

'You forget how unpopular we are as guests in your country. A man must be prepared for battle, even if he prefers to avoid it.'

'That's why you skulk in the woods?'

'That is why we seek to evade notice.'

She could hear a smile in his voice. He would be an attractive man, if he weren't a scoundrel.

No time was wasted by the men, who all knew their jobs. A fire was lit and after a meal of cold meat, bread, and ale from a skin with her cousin's mark on it, they settled around the fire to sleep, wrapped in their cloaks.

Cassia moved a little away, half wondering if it would be possible to slip into the forest and seek help. She had already rejected it when her arm was held in a fierce grip. 'Not so fast.'

The moment of indignation died swiftly. He had been right to suspect her. 'I wouldn't. I'd be too afraid of the wild animals.'

'Better the known beasts to the unknown.' His teeth flashed white in the firelight as he led her past the sleeping men. A blanket lay on the ground close to the fire and he pushed her down. With a glance at the surrounding mounds of fur and skin she complied, weary beyond words. She protested when he joined her, wrapping his heavy cloak over them both but it was half-hearted. If he intended to ravish her, he would get little pleasure from a woman more asleep than awake.

The following day was more of the same. Hard riding through forest lands, avoiding villages, slowing only to cross roads without being seen, stopping only to snatch a bite of bread and meat.

The third day was overcast and drear, with no sun to guide them. They had been travelling for hours when they stopped suddenly.

The older man pulled up beside Eiric. 'Are we lost, M'Lord?'

'Not yet.' He slid from the saddle and Cassia joined them, grateful for the chance to stretch.

To her surprise, the raider pulled a leather pouch from under his tunic. Inside was a shard of crystal, flat and almost the size of her palm. He held it up to the sky, turning slowly. The others watched impassively as if this were a common sight.

He nodded and slid the shard back into the pouch. 'We are off course, but not far.' He pointed with one long finger. 'This way is west.'

'Is it magic? Some kind of sorcerer's stone?'

His laughter filled the glade. 'Sorcery? No lass, it's a sunstone. Found only in the north of my homeland. Even on the darkest day it will find the light and show us the sun. Did you not see the sparkle when I held it high?'

She had, but hardly believed such a dull day would light a fire in the almost clear crystal.

There was no time for more for they had picked up the trail. There was no stopping for sleep. Instead she slept in the raider's arms, wrapped in his cloak, pinned close with her father's brooch as they rode through the night. She knew now why they travelled at such speed. He was chasing an errant bride. A woman promised to unite his kinfolk from across the sea with a family settled in the far north of her own land. It was a place she knew from her childhood, the language familiar as in a dream.

On the sixth day, they found them, lost deep in the mountains. The young man stood tall, sword in hand. The woman, barely more than a girl, was also fair and beautiful. A fitting bride for the raider for he was of some nobility, if his men were to be believed.

Cassia watched, anxious for the raider as he strode across the circle made by his men. The young man was not a match physically, but desperation shone in his eyes. He would fight for his lady.

'Stay back. Elinor is mine now.'

The girl stepped up beside her lover. 'I'm carrying his child, Eiric. You will have to kill us. We cannot go back.'

The raider signalled with one hand, the other on the hilt of his sword. 'I've no desire to kill today. I've come to deliver something you left behind.'

The older man dropped the wooden chest in front of the girl and stepped back.

'What is this?'

'Your dowry. You'll be needing it and by rights it's not mine. I've found another bride.'

The young woman stared. 'You release me?'

'I've no time for an unwilling bride.'

He stopped their gratitude with a raised hand. 'How did you come to be lost?'

The young man grunted. 'This hellish weather. No sun for days.'

'I have a wedding gift for you.' Eiric pulled the pouch from his tunic.

'Why would you give up such a rare treasure?'

Eiric commanded Cassia to approach. His thumb rubbed the yellow stone on her father's brooch. 'I have another such gem. It will show me the way to go.'

By nightfall, the runaway bride and her lover were gone, the men setting up camp in an adjacent clearing.

'Well, Cassia? Home to your kinfolk or home across the sea?'

She met his gaze, seeing in it all she never hoped for. 'Home across the sea.'

ROMANCE
WRITERS
of Australia

The Sunstone Inheritance

By

Fiona Marsden

'This isn't sunstone. It is some kind of crystal but not a gemstone.'

Ellie took back the clear shard and wrapped it in the scrap of silk. 'It says sunstone on the document that came with it. Lapis and sol.' She lay the photocopy of the original vellum on the counter. 'I had it translated. It says, 'This sunstone was a wedding gift to Elinor and Lorchan from Eric the Tortured.' Or it could be twisted. The professor thought he might be deformed. They used to name people the funniest things.'

'Perhaps the document doesn't pertain to that particular piece. But of course language has changed a lot in the last thousand years.' The jeweller pushed the paper back towards Ellie. 'I have someone coming in who knows more. A Norwegian.'

'A geologist?'

'No. A historian. A writer I believe. He was very interested in your crystal, Ms MacLaughlan. He has a collection of genuine sunstones. I'm expecting him any moment.'

The bell over the door chimed and Ellie turned. If Norwegian was code for blond Viking warrior in a three piece suit, this was her man. *If only.* He ducked his head coming through the door and she could bet he was used to having to compensate for his height. Close to two metres, and shoulders broad enough to be an American linebacker. And he wasn't even wearing pads.

The jeweller moved quickly around the counter to greet the giant. 'Mr Ericksson. You've come at the right time. Ms MacLaughlan owns the crystal I told you about.'

He looked at her with pale eyes, his fair brows bunched over his long nose in a frown that belied his words. 'A pleasure.'

His large hand swamped hers as she craned her neck to look up. She was average height but he made her feel like a leprechaun. Warmth swept along her skin from his touch, yet the speculative blue gaze chilled her from the inside out. She snatched back her hand and rubbed it on the fabric of her skirt. He unnerved her, and it wasn't just the size of him. 'I understand you're something of an expert on sunstone.'

'Not an expert. My family have collected pieces of sunstone jewellery for generations. Where I come from is one of the few places where it's plentiful.'

'Norway?'

'Yes.'

He hardly had an accent, though he sounded more British than Australian. 'Mr Bergin said you were interested in my sunstone, even though he thinks it isn't the real thing.'

'Very interested. May I take a look?'

The three of them moved to the counter and Ellie placed the flat package on the glass top. Ericksson hovered at her shoulder, way too close for comfort. Free of the wrapping, the crystal caught the light from the display case under the counter. Slivers of colour darted around the room, reflecting off the glasses of the old man and turning the Norwegian's cold eyes to a warm dark purple.

The silence said it all. It was beautiful. *He was beautiful.* Ellie dropped the fabric onto the counter and lay the stone on the pale silk. Now it was simply a flat crystal, slightly serrated on one edge.

'The silk looks old. Does it belong with the stone?'

She shivered at the touch of his breath on her cheek. 'It's not original. There's a leather pouch we believe is as old as the sunstone but it's very brittle so we leave it in the box. The silk was around the stone when my grandmother brought it out from Ireland in the sixties. It's parachute silk from the war.'

'Ireland? Do you know how long it's been in your family?'

'Records mentioning it go back to the fourteenth century.'

'The thirteen hundreds? Interesting.' His long finger stroked over the exposed crystal. 'It answers the description of the one I've been searching for.'

'You've been searching for this? But it's been in our family forever.'

'Not necessarily forever. It would have come from Norway originally. This type of crystal is found only in the north.'

Ellie searched his face. 'You mean the Vikings might have brought it to Ireland?'

'I'm almost certain.' His gaze pulled away and rested on the stone. 'A clear stone, the size of a woman's palm, with the spine of a wolf fish.'

Her chest tightened. It was a perfect description. 'It's been in our family for centuries. It's not like we stole it.'

'Are you certain?'

She pulled out the photocopied sheet. 'It was a gift. I have a document.'

He scanned the paper. 'This is in Latin. There is no date.'

'We know when they married.'

'This could have been written at any time after the fact. It means nothing.'

'What makes you so sure it was stolen?'

The jeweller was forgotten. It was only the two of them, duelling, eyes locked. 'The family stories tell of a runaway bride. She took with her the sunstone, a treasure of our house.'

'You think she stole it?'

'I cannot imagine my ancestor giving it away. They are rare and valuable.'

She couldn't breathe, her throat was tight.

'Are you all right?'

Sucking in air, Ellie nodded. 'You can't claim it. It's been hundreds of years. How would you even prove it?'

'I don't plan to claim it. I want to buy it.'

~ * ~

Her eyes wide, her mouth half open, she looked lost. Brand pushed down the unwelcome emotion that threatened to emerge. He did not want to feel sympathy for the girl. He was so close to restoring the last remnant of his family's heritage. Nothing, not even this redheaded girl with her unshuttered emerald eyes and freckled snub nose, would stop him.

'You can name your price. I realise its value.'

'No.' Her mouth, too wide for beauty but full and lush, firmed into a thin line.

He glanced at the jeweller, standing discretely in the background. 'I understood you wished to sell. Why else did you bring it to Mr Bergin?'

'I wanted it valued. For insurance. I never planned on selling it.'

The jeweller nodded. 'She asked for a value. I assumed it was for selling.' The man's eyes flicked over the girl in her shabby suit. It was neat and clean, probably her best, but the black fabric showed the rusty fading of frequent washing.

Brand addressed the girl. 'Will you consider it now?'

Her slightly crooked teeth bit at her lip. 'It's a family heirloom.'

'You can't eat an heirloom.'

Her face flushed. 'I'm not starving. I have a job. A good one.'

'Fine. But a little cash is always useful. A holiday, a new car. A better apartment.'

A stab in the dark but he hit home. Her chin lifted. 'I can manage perfectly well. Besides, you can't be sure it's the one your family owned.'

Coming out fighting. He liked this girl. *Woman.* She was probably older than she looked. The unruly curls and fresh face were misleading. There was a certain dignity that only comes with maturity.

'You said there was a leather pouch. Are there markings on the leather?'

Her brows drew together. 'There are. Very hard to see now. The surface is cracked and some bits have peeled off.'

'Perhaps you would care to show me.' He could see her about to refuse and raised his hand. 'In the interests of truth. It might help me to be sure. Or it could prove me wrong.'

The curl of her lips suggested she found that idea appealing. Obviously the liking wasn't mutual.

'It's at home.'

'Perhaps we could go there now. If you don't have other commitments.'

'I don't. But … I caught the bus in.' She obviously couldn't imagine him riding in a bus. Something he hadn't done since student days.

'I could drive you.'

She hesitated, looking at the watching jeweller.

'Mr Bergin will vouch for me.'

'How would he know?' She bit off what she was about to say.

'If I was a serial killer? It would be foolish of me to kill you now when someone knows we are together. An upright citizen who would naturally report all he knows to the police.'

The smile was reluctant, but there nevertheless. It transformed her face, lightening her eyes and revealing two dimples, a fraction away from the corners of her mouth. 'Well, you don't look stupid.' The emphasis on the *look* was accompanied by another smile. *She was teasing him?*

~ * ~

His car had that new smell, overlaying the scent of leather. She'd half expected him to be driving a Volvo, not an upmarket Mercedes Benz. It wasn't a small model, but he filled it with his presence all the same.

'My place isn't fancy. Just a bedsitter really.'

'Not my concern. I wish only to see your historical artefacts.'

He drove competently, talking easily. 'Could you tell me how you came to have the sunstone?'

'It's mine. My grandmother left it to me.'

'Specifically or with her property in general?'

'It was mentioned by name for me. The other things went to my uncle and his family.'

At a traffic light he turned to look at her. 'Why you?'

'Because of my name, I think. It's Elinor, but everyone calls me Ellie.'

'My name is Brand. It is not short for anything.'

No one would dare. 'Is it a family name?'

'On my mother's side. She felt Ericksson was enough to mark me as belonging.'

He smiled, showing even white teeth. Ellie looked away, disturbed by the attraction that sizzled through her insides.

'This is it.'

He parked at the front of the old fibro flats and looked at them with inscrutable eyes. 'Shall we go in?'

She led the way, unlocking the door of her room and casting a quick look around. At least it was clean. The space seemed to shrink as he turned slowly, assessing the room. She half expected some derogatory comment, but he shrugged off his jacket and hung it over one of the kitchen chairs. 'Shall we begin?'

Dropping her bag on the bench, Ellie knelt at the bed and pulled out an old suitcase. 'This is why I wanted an appraisal for insurance. I don't have anywhere special to keep valuable stuff.'

The chest was around the size of a shoe box but deeper, the aged timber darkened with handling over the centuries. There was a brass catch at the front but it was twisted and didn't quite work.

Brand expelled a sharp breath as she placed the box on the table. 'This came with your inheritance?'

'Yes. I haven't had a chance to work out what the engraving is. I was more worried about the crystal.'

'It is a runic alphabet. Viking writing.'

The tightness in her chest came back. 'Does that make it more likely you're right?'

'It's another link.'

He bent over the chest, his fingers tracing the straight lines of the carving. 'It is a bride chest. It would have held her dowry.'

'Does it say who it belonged to?' She had a horrible twisting feeling in her gut.

'Here it says *Elinor*.' He leaned closer. 'This carving of a dragon is covering some other word. Normally the groom's name would be here. Then to the side there is carving by a different hand. It says Lorchan.'

'Is that your runaway bride?'

His eyes gleamed with something hot and fierce as he met her gaze. 'I believe it is. This is remarkable. A real find. I never expected anything like this.' The way his hand stroked over the wood sent a prickle down her spine.

'Is it valuable?'

'Priceless.'

She wanted to flop down but a cold chill kept her standing. He wanted it, she could see it in the loving way he handled it. And before he'd even seen inside. Seen the leather pouch. 'On the open market? Or to you?'

He straightened, his face stiffening into a mask at her tone. 'It would be valuable to a museum, but even more so to us. To my family. The erased word looks like Eiric.'

'Why do you want it so much?'

'Our family lost our home and many of our heirlooms in the war when my grandfather was only a boy. I promised him I would find them and any others and restore them to the family.'

'So your sons can carry on?'

The corner of his mouth twitched. 'Theoretically. I have no sons, or daughters, at this point in time.'

'But you will have.'

'All being well. First I need to find a bride.' His narrowed gaze dropped to the bride chest, as if he was considering its value as a dowry. 'Are you planning on passing on the chest to your descendants?'

'Maybe. All being well. If I find a husband.' She echoed his words, suddenly hoping he wouldn't see them as a challenge.

The blue of his eyes darkened as he stared at her face. It felt like he was delving deep into her soul, the burning heat melting away her resistance.

He turned away, leaving her limp and weak kneed. 'Shall we examine the interior?' He sat on the chair with his jacket draped over it and opened the lid of the box. 'Do you mind?'

She could see he knew what he was doing. 'Go ahead.'

The pouch was wrapped in the same silk as the stone, to safeguard it. 'It probably should be in a museum or somewhere where it can be protected.'

'Possibly. The dry air here in Australia could be a blessing or a curse. At least the timber in the box hasn't dried or split.'

With careful hands, he unwrapped the parcel, lying the whole thing down without touching the leather. It seemed to take forever and then he just stared at it.

'Well?'

Brand leaned back in the chair, one hand tapping the table. 'You were right. The damage makes it almost impossible to see any detail. I might have more luck with a magnifying glass or if we take high resolution photographs.' He pointed to the centre front of the pouch. 'There is something there that could be the symbol for sun but I wouldn't like to stake my life on it. It's quite likely Viking manufacture. The leather is probably reindeer hide.'

'Rudolph?'

A soft snort almost turned into a laugh. 'Maybe his great-great grandfather.'

'What now?' She hardly knew whether she wanted it to be true or not. If it was, he would want to buy it. If not, he would go away and she would never see him again.

'I think we need to run more tests. Do you have any objection?'

She could feel her body relaxing. It wasn't over. He would have to stay in contact until the tests came back. 'Will it be expensive?'

'I'm the one requesting them, so the responsibility for any costs is mine.' He smiled without humour.

'What if you're wrong? You will have wasted your money.'

The disturbing smile widened. 'I don't think I am.'

Picking up the chest, he tipped it to look at the hinges. A rattle from inside the box startled both of them. He placed it back on the table. 'What else is in here?'

'Nothing, apart from the silk Gran lined the bottom with.'

She watched him pull the fabric out. There was a lot of it, padding the contents against the rigours of travel from Ireland. Together they looked at the base of the interior. It was lined with long strips of a lighter wood. One had come loose, lying askew across the others.

Lifting it out, Brand held it to the light coming through the window, 'There are markings.'

Her heart kicked over a notch. 'Viking runes?'

'Yes.' He studied them carefully and then laughed. 'It reads like a grocery list. Two bags of flour, one skin of ale, two of wine.'

Disappointment soured her stomach. 'Is that all? What does it say on the other side?'

He was still smiling as he turned over the thin, roughly smoothed piece of timber. 'It's something different.' His smile faded as he focused on the markings. 'A contract. Or rather the dissolution of a marriage contract. Signed by Eiric Skellan. My ancestor. There are remnants of wax here, an official seal possibly.'

'Why on a piece of wood?' She would have thought he'd be happy about it, not frowning fiercely, his brow knotted in that way he had.

'Paper wasn't an option and vellum was expensive and not always available. Using strips of wood was quite common for our Viking ancestors. Runes are easy to carve on soft timber.'

He was pulling the other pieces from the base of the chest and lying them carefully on the table. 'Some of these are lists, the original contents of the dowry, but there are two more that are significant.'

She stood close beside him as his finger traced the words. '*I give this sunstone to Elinor of Jorvik,*' he glanced up. 'Present day York in England. *In token of good faith on her wedding to Lorchan of the Kingdom of Dublin. Signed, Eirik Skellan. Witnessed by two others.*'

'So it was a gift.'

'And I have no claim.' He silently replaced the pieces of timber into the chest.

So that was it. 'I'm so sorry.'

He wriggled his broad shoulders as if to dislodge something. 'Perhaps it is all for the best.' His blue eyes captured hers. 'Now we stand together with no obligation, nothing hanging from the past.'

'Is that a good thing?' Her heart was beating faster with something like … hope.

'We are now only a Viking seeking a bride and you are a woman with a desirable dowry.'

She couldn't hold back the smile to match his. 'How desirable?'

'Do you wish to come to dinner so we can discuss the matter?' He put out his hand.

With no hesitation Ellie placed hers into it. It felt right. 'I do.'

Lights Will Guide You Home

By

Michelle Skidmore

It had been one month, twelve days, and approximately fifty-three minutes.

Eamann knew he should not be counting, not really, since there was still so much work to do—a tremendous amount, truly—but he could no more stop himself from counting the passing time than he could stop the two moons from rising. Forty-two days that Eamann had to push through without the laughter, teasing grins and words, that knowing look in her cerulean eyes, whispered nothings, and lips pressed against sweet lips.

The days were longer now, the snow melting, flowers springing from their icy prison as winter reluctantly shifted from the mountain fortress of Whitehaven.

He shrugged deeper into his fur-ruffed coat, wishing armour did more to keep out the chill drifting through his study. Even with the door solidly closed, the gusts found their way through the slit windows. The candles flickered. Their ominous dance mirrored the shadows within him.

Mithrain, how could the sun still rise and set when she was no longer beneath it? The other advisors of the Luminariate expected him to carry on with his tasks as if nothing had changed. Curse it, *everything* had changed.

Eamann didn't want any part of this, he didn't want to train the experienced soldiers and the bumbling recruits and teach battle tactics, or fortify their walls; he wanted to be able to cross the yard and take Liah into his arms, to kiss the sheer life out of her regardless of who was watching, to hug her until she scowled and complained that he always wore his 'blasted armour', rubbing her cheek where it'd rammed into his chestplate. He wanted the flirting, the little glances at each other across the war table, the stolen moments on the battlements between missions. He wanted her here, planted on top of his desk, legs swinging, tempting him from his never-ending paperwork.

But he was the Commander of the Luminariate's soldiers. What he wanted didn't matter.

He dropped his head back. The Luminariate. A force rising up to defend Valendor from the dangers of dark magic and heretics, a purpose transcending kingdom and empire. They were the light of hope for the people. And the people sorely needed hope.

A blood mage, Lazarus, would see all of Valendor slaughtered by his demon army in his bid to become a god. If they failed to defeat him … Mithrain, don't even think it. Liah was their light. Her kindness, compassion, and belief in equality for all, be they human, elf, or dwarf, mage or warrior, drew people to her. So she became the Luminariate's First Mage, solidifying their ranks to meet this threat.

No, what he wanted certainly didn't matter.

His gloved hand fisted around the quill, threatening to snap the fragile feather. How did those left behind move on?

He had no real time to grieve—Lazarus was still out there, biding his time, waiting to lash out. Perhaps even now, the rogue mage marched on them, demon army at his heels, striking while they reeled from this unthinkable loss. He needed to pull himself together, rally his men, and see to their defences …

Or he could hide in the shadows, and wallow in the loss of the woman he loved.

Move on?

Ha. What a fantasy. An illusion by those who knew nothing of loss.

Who knew nothing of the torment ripping through his chest.

But he had a duty. To her. To their friends. To every man, woman, and child fleeing the atrocities and death brought by this horde. To every fallen man. To Valendor. The strict training of twenty-odd years kept him from completely losing focus. He would do his duty.

Weeping wouldn't help now.

Nothing would.

He refocused on his paperwork. Tried to, at least. It swam before his eyes. He rubbed his lids. Right. The sodding report he couldn't concentrate on. There was simply so much to do. He needed to write an accounting of the Luminariate and their allied troops, of material losses, of intelligence gathered and supplies taken. He yawned. A note to Empress Anaïs of Ardentes, thanking her for the three legions of knights she'd sent. He still had to … assess the manifest of gathered resources and … and recovered arms.

He needed to … Needed to …

Eamann didn't notice when his head hit the desk.

~ * ~

It wasn't the first time a heated debate erupted over the war table. Mithrain's breath, were they all intent on sending Liah to her death? He wouldn't have it! This latest mission was … was … utterly inconceivable. Gabriella and Elodie should know better.

Oh, the rational part of his mind understood; they needed to see if these men and women shored up in the wilds of the Draggr Forest could be persuaded to their cause—they needed all the help they could get. Time was running out fast. Elodie's spies reported Lazarus marched on an old dwarven city in search of some ancient crafted artefact, putting him one step closer to his goal of immortality. They had to stop him at all costs. Which meant more men. Liah's compassion made her perfect for the task.

He immediately refused. Those men could just as easily turn on her! They were betrayers who'd abandoned the kingdom of

107

Llewynroc; where did their loyalty lie? He found this gamble questionable at best.

But it seemed he was outvoted by three women.

Eamann followed Liah to her quarters. She was to leave on the morrow. He batted one of her wind chimes out of the way, ignoring their gentle melody. 'Liah, I implore you: please reconsider.'

'It's not far,' she soothed, flicking a white-blonde lock over her shoulder. 'I will be back in a matter of days.'

He didn't want her to go. Especially not without him, without his sword to protect her. They could not afford to lose her. *He* could not lose her.

She bit her lip. 'You're looking at me with those amber puppy-dog eyes again.'

He started. 'I … am?'

'Yes, and it's adorable.'

'Good. Then look at me, and reconsider.'

'Eamann …'

'I don't want you to go.'

She closed the gap between them, resting a hand on his armour, right above his heart. 'I'm sorry. This … is bigger than us. We knew that from the start.'

Duty before love—he'd hoped to never have to make that decision.

He drew back. Her hand fell from his chest, and her eyes clouded over. 'Forgive me. I … know that. My duty is to remain here, train the men for whatever great battle lies ahead. And you cannot shirk your duty as First Mage.' His features softened. 'No matter how much I might wish you to.'

He slipped a golden ring from his pinkie and slid it onto her finger. The topaz-orange stone caught the glint of the sun through her open balcony doors. It seemed to shine with a holy light. 'I want you to take this. The sunstone, it's a family heirloom. May its light guide you home.'

'Eamann … thank you.' Her eyes glittered.

He couldn't resist. What began as a chaste brushing of lips quickly descended into a frenzy of unrestrained emotions. It took great effort for Eamann to pull back. Her slightly-swollen lips begged for more. Mithrain's breath, her *lips*.

'Celestine, preserve me,' he groaned. He gave her a stern look. 'I'm appointing you an extra unit of soldiers.'

She smiled sweetly, that seductive dimple making a brief appearance. 'If that will make you feel better.'

'Be careful. Losing you …'

'I understand. But all will be well.'

She reached up to pull his face down to hers once more. 'I love you, Eamann.' She kissed him, then leant her forehead against his. He inhaled her scent, orange blossoms and woman.

'Mithrain watch over you.'

The next day, he watched her ride through the gates of Whitehaven, unease stirring in his gut. Twenty of his best men accompanied her, along with their companions, warrior Sigrid and dwarven rogue Kendric. As she said, all would be well.

~ * ~

They were late. Eamann paced his study, muscles tense. A matter of days, she said. What could have delayed them? It took all his willpower not to ride out and find why they'd been waylaid.

Hooves pounded in the courtyard below. His head shot up. At last! He peered out a loophole, searching for the white-blonde hair he liked to run his fingers through. His stomach dropped.

He wrenched the door open and ran, his lungs stinging with the cold, dry air. He stumbled into the chaos below.

Only two of his men accompanied Sigrid and Kendric. They all wore grim expressions, covered in sweat and blood.

Where was Liah?

Her mare stood off to the side, flanks heaving and slick with sweat. She looked exhausted. Her reins hung low from the bridle, her saddle smeared with … something. She skittered as he neared, but stilled under his hand. Closer now, he could see the saddle clearly. *Blood.*

'No. Mithrain, no …' His throat closed.

He barely heard Elodie's sharp command. 'Sigrid, tell us.'

'Those *traitors* were experimenting with volatile magic,' Sigrid ground out, her Northern accent thick with distress.

'They had magic?' the Spymaster echoed in disbelief.

'Yes. They unleashed their weapon upon us—and it *exploded*.' Kendric snorted. 'It didn't injure men—it eviscerated them.'

'Nothing was left of those the magic touched. The horses bolted in all directions, more explosions following. We fought against the remaining men. When it was done … we could not find her.'

Eamann's jaw clenched. 'Then you didn't look hard enough.'

'We did, Commander. We spent days searching the area, hoping to find even a trace of her. But there was nothing to find. She was … gone.'

~ * ~

Bam! Bam! Bam!

Eamann blinked bleary eyes, throwing up a hand to block the morning sun streaming through the windows. Fog clouded his usual alertness. He'd fallen asleep at his desk. Again. Mithrain, his *head.* What was the point of sleep when you woke feeling even worse?

Sigrid and Kendric barged in, clearly tiring of waiting on him. He'd wager he had an imprint of his gauntlet on his cheek. Wonderful.

The dwarf chuckled. 'Well, don't you look like a bloody ray of sunshine?'

Sigrid's brows lowered. 'You need to sleep. In a bed.'

'I'll sleep when I'm dead,' Eamann growled.

'Of all the stupid, stubborn …' She swallowed the words.

He knew what he looked like—he owned a looking glass. Pale skin, dark circles beneath his eyes, and a sunken quality about his face. Sandy hair dishevelled from clutching the strands hard enough to cause enough pain to keep him grounded—and to punish himself.

If Liah were here, she'd be chewing his arse out like these two.

His heart stuttered in his chest, almost crippling him with its ache.

'Have you at least been eating?' Sigrid persisted. 'I cannot recall seeing you do so.'

'Not … really.' He rubbed the back of his neck, heat flooding his cheeks. 'I can't keep much down.'

Kendric crossed his arms. 'Keep that up, Blondie, and we'll be scraping you off the floor to lead the Luminariate forces.'

'I'm fine.'

Sigrid pinned him with a hard stare, obsidian eyes brooking no refusal. 'I expect to see you in the main hall for breakfast within the half hour.' The two swept out of his study without as much as a by your leave.

Eamann shook his head, but the fog refused to clear. Echoes of his dreams swirled through his mind unchecked.

Whitehaven had been subdued following the survivors' return. A state of mourning had fallen, many in disbelief. Their First Mage, their hope, gone? She couldn't have fallen, not before the final battle.

Eamann recalled little of that first week, stumbling around the fortress like one of the undead. The copious amounts of ale he'd consumed did nothing to ease the jagged wound in his chest. Only his sense of duty kept him putting one foot in front of the other.

He should've gone with her. Been where he was needed and where he needed to be.

He paused, taking several deep breaths to get his emotions under control.

It didn't work. The pain beneath his breastbone throbbed, demanding release.

With a roar of despair, he swiped everything from his desk. Small boxes tumbled hard, glass bottles smashed, papers fluttered in their wake. He stood there, chest heaving. His fists clenched and unclenched at his side. Enough!

He stormed from the study. Long strides ate up the ground, heading across the courtyard, through the gardens to Celestine's shrine. Refugees and soldiers scattered out of his way, cowering at his glare. Now he was scaring people. Good. It matched his mood perfectly.

The small shrine was empty. The door slammed behind him, shutting him within these stone walls, in a sudden, eerie silence. The statue of Celestine rose above him, the Maiden's hands stretched out in an entreaty. Her bowed head seemed to stare at him as he stood before her, vision hazy from the scented candles at her feet. Or so he told himself.

He drew his sword, hilt gripped tight, and brandished it at the statue. He cared not that such an act was blasphemy in this sacred shrine. 'Why didn't you save her, Celestine?' he shouted at the stone. Rage sizzled through him, borne of the desolation twisting his gut.

'*Why?* Answer me! Or Mithrain … It cannot have been your will that she die! I cannot believe that! That you would desert her, when she needed you most. When she … No …'

The hot sting of tears made their way down his cheeks. He sank to his knees, supporting himself on his blade, throat convulsing. He couldn't breathe, couldn't … He squeezed his eyes shut. Finally managed a deep, shuddering breath.

'Mithrain, you should've protected her. You should've … You …' A sob caught in his throat. '*I* should've protected her. *I failed her.*'

On the floor of the shrine, before the statue of Great Celestine, the Commander let loose his misery.

~ * ~

Eamann lifted his head out of his hands when a call came up from the courtyard below. More trouble? Couldn't they leave him in peace? No, time continued on. Stomping mercilessly on his sorrow, he heaved himself off the hard ground. He had to focus on protecting those who remained.

'Commander!' His lieutenant ran into the shrine, eyes wide, out of breath. Only belatedly did the man remember to pound a fist to his chest in a salute. 'Sir, you better come quick.' And then he was off.

Alarmed, Eamann threw off his weariness and sprinted after Lieutenant Finnar. He knew his red, swollen eyes would attest to his foolishness in the shrine; he would rather his men didn't see his weakness, but he had little choice. What had gone wrong? It would take a dragon descending on Whitehaven to unsettle his lieutenant like this. Or was Lazarus making his move? Mithrain, let the demon army not be on their doorstep.

He reached the stairs leading to the courtyard, and assessed the madness below. His eyes widened. He blinked. Blinked again. It couldn't be …?

In the centre of the confusion, she stood still, staring up at him. Her face was smudged with dirt and blood, her hair a tangled mess. No, it couldn't be her. His body shuddered as magic swirled around his senses—*her* magic. Hope pounded in his chest.

He staggered down the steps, only to halt on the landing. No. He would not be deceived by this illusion. He'd confronted trickery like this before. But that magic, it *had* to be hers … He reacted this way to no other's power.

She ran up the stairs to him, wincing with each step, meeting him on the landing. Cerulean eyes greedily lapped him up.

He swallowed. 'Are you … are you real?'

Those lips, lips he *knew*, quirked at the corners. 'I hurt too much not to be.'

The noose loosened around his heart.

He bit the tip of a glove and yanked his hand from its depths, then tore off the other. He needed to feel her warmth, skin against skin. He cupped her cheek—it was cold from the harsh wind, but still held an underlying warmth.

Liah.

'Thank Mithrain you're alive,' he whispered.

She closed her eyes, leaning into his palm, like a flower seeking the sun's heat.

'But how …?' He couldn't even finish around the lump in his throat.

She moistened her lips. 'Turns out the traitors' magic was a portal. Or rather, more of a distortion in the physical plane. It spat me out in the middle of a forest. Along with all the other men displaced by the spell. Eamann … I barely got away. I crawled to a safe hollow in the forest, too afraid of being defenceless to use all my magic at once with a healing spell. And hunting by magic is no easy feat. All I could think of was getting back to you. I didn't know where I was, which way to go … Then this showed me the way.'

He reluctantly tore his gaze from her sweet face. His sunstone ring *glowed* on her finger. 'I … don't recall that possessing magic.'

'It's no magic I've seen before.'

Eamann brushed a finger against the cool stone. The orange light pulsed brighter, encompassing them in its radiance. It reacted to him? No, not him. *Them.*

'I was lost. I thought of you … and its light guided me home.' She exhaled, and looked up at him, eyes glistening with unshed tears. Her voice cracked as she whispered, 'I'm finally home.'

Right there, in front of the crowd of onlookers, the Commander pulled their First Mage into his arms, burying his nose in her hair. He didn't care if his armour dug into her, he just needed to hold her tight. She was here, safe and whole and *home*. If he could, he would kiss Mithrain himself for such a blessing.

She wrapped her arms tightly around his waist and sank further into his embrace. 'I'm sorry if I worried you. Forgive me?'

'Always.'

Treasure and Trust

By

Victoria Steele

It's me or the stone.

Here I am, hanging by my fingertips over a chasm down to God knows where and my fate rests in the hands of a man I'm not even sure I can trust.

As I try to pull myself up again, biceps straining, feet scrabbling against the rock face, I can feel the dirt beneath my hands beginning to crumble away. I scream again, wondering if he can hear me. And if he can, whether he would come anyway. Below me, the ground groans and shrieks like all the souls in hell as the world splits apart. If he's going to choose me, he'd better hurry.

I know he wants me—that's been obvious since he walked into my flat three days ago with a proposition I should have turned down—but he's been chasing treasure all his life. So the question is, which does he want more?

~ * ~

It was a Thursday morning like any other that Flynn McCormack knocked on my door and turned my world on its head. Allow me to introduce myself—Eve Campbell. I like to call myself an Egyptologist, though some people have used the word *grave-robber* to describe my profession. Some people can be unkind. I find things of value, things of beauty, things that have been lost from sight for thousands of years, and allow people to enjoy them again. If I choose to do that for those who have plenty of cash to splash around, is that so great a sin?

But I digress … When I opened my front door, Flynn was the last person I expected to see. Rangy, unshaven and lounging against the porch wall in his usual laid-back fashion. King of his world.

'Hi Eve. Miss me?' Given that the last time I saw him was when he ran out on me in a seedy Cairo hotel room, cheating me out of a tidy pile of cash, I assumed the question was rhetorical.

'Well, well aren't you just the bad penny?' I replied coolly, trying to push away the memories that crowded into my mind at the sight of him. The sultry Cairo heat, the tangle of sheets on our bodies, the taste of salt on his skin. 'What brings you sniffing around my door?'

'I have a job for you, if you're interested.' He paused, his fingers tapping the door frame. 'You know it would be the polite thing to invite me in.'

'A job?' I repeated, not moving from the doorway, despite the fact that the warmth of his body was disturbingly tangible. 'You're asking for my help?'

Flynn smiled slowly. A tingle ran down my spine. Flynn McCormack has a smile that can do things to a girl—and he knows it. He was turning it on full force here. I couldn't afford to let my guard down.

Still, curiosity got the better of me. I stepped aside and let him in.

'I need to get access to the tombs below the Temple of Sekhmet in Dahshur,' he said, taking a seat on my battered couch. 'So far, despite my best efforts at persuasion, I haven't been able to find anyone who will oblige. However, I believe you have some contacts there who can open doors, literally. Am I right?' He cocked his head and regarded me with a languid golden-eyed stare.

'Perhaps I might,' I replied, sitting opposite rather than beside him. Some distance needed to be preserved, for my own clarity of mind. 'What's in it for me?'

'Apart from the pleasure of my company?'

I narrowed my eyes, so Flynn reached into the bag beside him and took out a small bundle of dirty cloth. He placed it on the table and slowly unwrapped it to reveal a golden object of obvious antiquity and value. I bent forward to take a closer look.

It was an amulet in the shape of a lion's head. Beautifully crafted and inlaid with lapis lazuli, it had evidently been buried with someone who had some coin. Despite my better judgement, my interest was piqued.

'I understand it came from the tomb of one of the 12th dynasty pharaohs,' Flynn went on. 'It was originally discovered in 1926, but recently came into my possession through a combination of good fortune and a particularly violent game of poker. It is a depiction of the goddess Sekhmet herself, probably intended to protect the pharaoh from his enemies in the afterlife.'

I reached out my hand. 'May I?' He passed the piece across.

As I examined the amulet I could see that, although it was undoubtedly beautiful, it was far from perfect. At the base of the piece, below the lion-goddess's chin, sat a gaping hole about the size of the ball of my thumb.

I handed it back to him. 'You want the gemstone,' I guessed. 'But how can you even know what you are looking for?'

'As Sekhmet was a daughter of Ra, the sun god, I suspect it will be a sunstone—not a particularly valuable stone in itself but as part of this, priceless. I want to find that stone.'

I leant my elbow on the arm on my chair and rested my chin on my hand.

'Even if I could help you, and I'm not saying I can, why on earth should I trust you?'

He leant back and crossed his legs at the ankles. 'Is this about Cairo? Believe me, I did you a favour there.'

It didn't seem that way to me. The night before we were to meet up with the contacts who would hand over the spoils we had been hunting for, I had let myself mix pleasure with business. I woke the next morning to find Flynn gone, along with my share of the treasure. The offence of that was compounded by the ignominious fact that I had started to feel more than I should have for the scoundrel. I would not make that mistake again.

'Really?' I replied dryly. 'But getting back to my initial point, what's in it for me?'

He shifted in his seat. 'Well I'm sure there's plenty of other loot there—whatever you can carry is yours.'

'Flynn, you know as well as I do that most of the tombs in Dahshur were picked clean in the 1920s. You'll have to do better than that.'

He began wrapping the amulet.

'Fine, whatever I get for the completed amulet, I'll split with you 70/30.'

'Try again.'

'60/40?'

'Halves or nothing, Flynn. After all, half of priceless is still pretty good, right?'

Grudgingly he extended his hand and I shook it, wondering as I did so if I was making a deal with the devil.

~ * ~

My contact in Dahshur was not inclined to be helpful, at least at first.

'No, Miss Campbell, it is too dangerous. The earthquakes …'

In the preceding days, as we had been travelling across the country, a few small tremors were recorded, not an unusual occurrence in this region—I didn't see it as that great a problem.

'Please Abdul, we won't be down there for long,' I said, acutely aware of Flynn's eyes on me. It would be mortifying to have come all this way only to fail him at the first hurdle.

Abdul lowered his voice. 'The tremors, Miss … some say it is the wrath of Anubis. Too many have been disturbing the peace of the dead of late. I beg you, go home. It is folly to anger the gods.'

I wasn't about to give up that easily. Surreptitiously, I held up a purse of coins, hoping to sweeten the deal.

'Come on Abdul, my friend and I want an hour in the temple at most. We'll be gone before you know it. Anubis won't even know we were here.'

He frowned but the lure of the purse was stronger than his faith in the end. And, I daresay, the few choice pieces of information I had about him which he was keen to keep quiet probably played their part too. Contacts with a seedy past are the best kind. In any case, he cracked and led us down to the gates.

As we stepped inside and descended the steps, a small aftershock trembled through the room, sending trickles of sand and dust down the walls.

'This better be worth it,' I muttered, steadying myself against the block wall until the shuddering subsided.

'If you want to wait up top, I'm happy to go alone,' Flynn offered, shining a torch beam around us looking for the way into the main chamber.

'Oh I bet you are,' I snapped in reply, jumping down next to him. 'No way buddy—fool me twice, shame on me.'

He gave an exasperated sigh and set off into the tunnel, and I followed. No way was he leaving me behind again.

Five minutes of loaded silence later, my frayed temper got the better of me.

'While we're on the subject, when we get back home, how about you give me my half of what you got in Cairo two years ago.'

Flynn stopped and turned to face me. 'Trust me,' he replied, 'you don't want any of what I got in Cairo.'

I was about to argue, but his expression made me pause. It was grim, haunted.

'Flynn?' I said softly. 'Tell me what happened.'

He exhaled and leant back against the stone wall behind him.

'I left you at the hotel that morning because I suspected we might be walking into a trap. Turned out I was right. I also thought I'd be able to outsmart them—unfortunately on that count I was wrong. A gang of four guys worked me over and left me for dead in a prison cell, where I spent the next six weeks.'

He raised his face to mine. 'I don't even want to think about what they would have done to you if you'd been with me, Eve.' And though I knew he could lie with the best of them, this time I believed him.

'If you thought it was a trap, why didn't you just say?'

'Because I knew you would never have stayed behind willingly. You didn't trust me then any more than you do now.'

He was right, of course. I wouldn't have let him go alone and risked missing out. It seemed I'd dodged a bullet—or rather he'd taken one for me. I owed Flynn McCormack a lot of things and the first was an apology.

But the words had hardly formed on my lips when the ground shifted beneath our feet again.

'Come on,' he said, 'let's find this tomb before Anubis gets any more pissed off.'

As we ventured further in, the tunnel grew narrower and the rocky floor began to slope. I watched Flynn angle his shoulders to fit between some of the smaller gaps as he led the way. Things had been about to get serious, at least for me, before that night in Cairo, and I was sharply reminded of all that I had been drawn to back then. His determination, his humour, that killer smile—there was altogether too much to like about the guy. Perhaps it wasn't too late?

'You got any plans for dinner tonight, Flynn?' I asked casually, as we stepped out into a large chamber, perhaps twenty feet high. I shone my torch around the walls and counted four doorways. We'd need to split up if we wanted to do this fast.

Flynn raised an eyebrow. 'Nothing in particular,' he replied. Those dark-lashed golden eyes regarded me with amusement, giving me a warm rush even in the half-light. 'Why do you ask?'

'Oh, I know a good place in town. My shout. You know, just to, ah, make up for the whole Cairo thing.'

He smiled, and I thought I detected genuine affection in that smile, which was something far more attractive than any amount of sex appeal. I swallowed and tried to stay casual but my heart raced. Oh God yes, this could really go somewhere.

'I believe I would enjoy that very much, Eve.' He brushed a thumb along my cheekbone and I took a deep breath, anticipating a kiss I had relived more times than I cared to admit.

'But right now,' he went on, stepping back a pace, 'I think we need to focus on finding this stone and getting the hell out of here.'

He was right of course, but it took me a few moments to clear my fuddled head and see sense. *Tonight*, I told myself, *wait 'til tonight*. And this time it would be different.

'Pick a door … ladies first,' Flynn offered, turning back to survey the room. I chose the first on the left and set off, clambering over the rocks and debris and giant blocks of sandstone that littered the chamber. Flynn turned right and disappeared into door number 2 on that side.

I entered the room and took a look around. It had obviously been picked over many times since the 1920s when Egyptology had been at its peak. My torch beam showed little but rubble. In one corner a sarcophagus lay open, so I climbed over for a closer look, but could see nothing inside but sand. Nevertheless, I started sifting.

After about fifteen minutes of this, I began to see the enormity of our task. We were looking for a stone about an inch long, which might not even be here, in a desert of sand. It was the definition of hopeless. I straightened up and was making my way back to tell Flynn as much, when a quake took hold, stronger than any we had felt previously. I balanced myself against the doorway as showers of sand and small rocks cascaded around me and the ground beneath me shook. It was definitely time to go.

As I entered the main chamber, I heard Flynn's voice.

'Eve, do you have a chisel? I think I've found something.'

It was just as I stopped to rifle through my shoulder bag that the ground beneath my feet gave a massive lurch and fell away completely.

~ * ~

So this is how I came to be in my current predicament. I can't see the door through which Flynn disappeared in the darkness and I no longer have a torch. I scream again and kick frantically for a foothold but my fingers are slipping. It's too late. He's not coming.

Just as my grip begins to fail, I feel Flynn's fingers clamp around my wrist.

'Eve, grab my hand! Hurry!'

Using the last of my strength, I fling my other hand up to find his and he hauls me over the edge. Safe in his arms, I feel his heart racing and realise he is shaking, almost as much as I am. His lips find mine, and though I want the kiss to go on forever, I have to make do with intense but brief as the room is still shaking far more than either of us. Flynn shines his torch towards the stairs we came in by, which are mercifully unobstructed, and he pulls me to my feet.

'Wait,' I pant, glancing back towards door number 2. 'Did you find it?'

Flynn shoots me an incredulous look. 'Are you nuts? Come on, we have to get out of here!'

We bolt up the stairs and out into the light, spluttering and coughing as the dust billows out with us. In our wake, the Temple of Sekhmet caves in upon itself, as Anubis reclaims the dead.

~ * ~

That night, when the world is still and the breeze stirs the curtains in our little hotel room, I run my hand over Flynn's chest and ask sleepily, 'Are you sorry you didn't get what you came for?'

His voice rumbles against my ear. 'Who says I didn't?'

I lift my head to look him in the face, half expecting him to produce the stone from his ear, magician-style, and he laughs.

'No, I didn't get the sunstone Eve, but I think I can say this trip has still been extremely rewarding.'

'Priceless?' I purr as I nestle my head back down.

'Exactly.'

The Healing Gift

By

Camille Taylor

'Not only am I about to marry Christy, the most beautiful woman in the room, I'm also pleased to announce that in a few short months I'll be a father.'

He didn't. He did. The man showed no courtesy for her. He could at least given her a heads up. The room spun, a whistle began in her ears as blood raced to her cheeks. Kara Davies shifted uncomfortably on her feet, trying to ignore the blatant stares of her colleagues. They all knew she'd dated Adam Parker, and when they had broken up, and were no doubt doing the math in their heads.

She wasn't sure why it bothered her. It's not like she still loved him. Her heart may have been broken but no longer. All that remained was anger and embarrassment. He'd humiliated her time and time again. Would there be no end?

She waited for the celebratory sips when attention finally diverted from her to their champagne, and then slipped from the room out onto the balcony overlooking the sparkling lights of Darling Harbour.

'That no good, cheating son of a … aargh.' She stomped her high-heeled foot.

'Anyone I know?'

A strangled gasp escaped as she turned, spotting the shadowed figure leaning against the maroon brick of the building. In a lithe move, the man pushed away and stepped toward her.

'Mr Dalton, my apologies. I didn't realise anyone was out here.'

Fresh embarrassment washed over her, her little meltdown witnessed by a senior partner at the firm. Thankfully, the soft glow escaping from the office through the large ceiling to floor windows hid her heated cheeks.

'I'm not one for parties, though I'm made to attend. I see can why you escaped. Never did like Parker, hasn't a decent bone in his body.'

Kara ducked her head, humiliation wafting around her like a dark cloud. He knew. Why that surprised her she wasn't sure. There were no secrets at Walsh, Hamilton and Dalton.

Tears pricked her eyes. Everyone knew what he'd done to her and looked at her with pity. Being deceived and dumped was bound to send sympathy her way. Why she felt particularly embarrassed with Brendan Dalton knowing she wasn't sure.

Shrugging, she found herself fiddling with the twinkling Christmas decorations hanging joyfully from the railing. What could she say? She'd thought she'd been in love with him once. Three years they'd dated. Two and a half years he'd lied.

'How are you holding up?'

'Like I want to melt into the floor and disappear.'

Biting her lip, Kara immediately regretted her honesty. What must he be thinking? Probably wondering if she was unstable. That's all she needed.

He studied her face carefully. Kara stilled beneath his perusal wondering what he saw. Probably nothing good judging by the look in his serious brown eyes. She lifted her chin and steeled her spine. Her heart of its own accord beat ferociously in her chest as she waited, nerves eating away at her. She couldn't help but notice the lushness of his lips, the cleft in his chin or the errant chocolate curl which rested against his forehead.

Amusement filled his voice. 'If you did I'd be alone again.'

She jolted when he swept away a lock of hair that blew across her face. A simple touch yet she felt as if she'd been electrified.

'I uh … um.' Unable to hold his penetrating gaze, she found herself staring at his chest, wrapped deliciously in a forest green shirt. The loose end of his tie hung limply over his broad chest, one good gust of wind away from disappearing down twenty floors to the street below.

'I have something for you.'

'M me?'

Rising panic choked from within. Good Lord, please don't let it be a redundancy letter. That's all her crappy year needed. She gripped the railing, her knees not quite steady.

He handed her a small jewellery box. She bit her lower lip as she stared at it, unsure if she should open it.

'I apologise for the lateness. I was called away on a case and was in London before I realised I'd forgotten to place it beneath the tree. It breaks the rules of Secret Santa I know but I guess it doesn't matter now.'

She'd not considered a senior partner may have gotten her name. Or that they even participated. When 'Santa' had ho-ho-ho'd through the office emptying his bag, she'd assumed hers had been lost or an uneven number of people had played. Truthfully, she'd thought it fitting that even Santa had forgotten her. That appeared to be her luck.

'Are you going to open it?'

'Oh, yes of course.'

She lifted the lid and stared down at the pretty gold ring nestled gently within the protective cushioning. The Harbour Bridge's light reflected back in the pale amber stone.

Kara sucked in a breath. 'It's beautiful.'

'It's a sunstone. My sister is into the whole crystal new age thing and owns a shop. They promote emotional healing among other things. I thought of you when I saw it. I figured after all you've been through, you could use some healing.'

She stared at him, speechless. The gift was ... wonderful. He'd put a lot of thought into the selection. She swallowed hard, feeling emotional. It had been a while since someone had showed her such kindness. She was becoming familiar with the feeling of being used and mortified.

'Thank you. Although truth be told I was just expecting a novelty coffee mug but this is ... thank you.'

'You're welcome. Anything to bring back that smile of yours. You have a beautiful smile. I've missed it.'

Her heart thumped in her chest. He had? She'd never noticed him much before, except as her boss, a good-looking man she rarely conversed with in her paralegal role. He'd been pleasant enough to greet in the corridor but she'd been swept up in her blossoming romance with Adam, and had been lucky to remember to look both ways before crossing the street let alone realise the world was full of decent, honest men.

It was strange to hear a man admit he'd missed her smile. He was sweet. The admission melted her heart, especially after the crappy year she'd been having.

'I haven't had a lot to smile about.' Her soft voice went no farther than his ears before being swallowed by the gentle breeze that teased her hair. There was no point ignoring the truth. She'd been made to look a fool. That was the worst thing. The moment she'd heard about his infidelity all the love she'd borne had died but how he'd flaunted his new relationship around the office had been more than she could bear.

'I'm sorry.'

'So am I.'

'Do you love him still?'

Kara shook her head. 'No. Maybe I never did. No one in love could fall out so easily. But the betrayal hurt. As does the humiliation and it appears he has no regard as to my feelings.'

Brendan leaned his arms on the balcony railing, staring out at the glistening waves in the packed harbour. New Year's Eve in Sydney always managed to draw a crowd with the spectacular display of fireworks. Kara only hoped her self-recriminations and sorrow didn't dampen her spirits too much that she couldn't enjoy it.

'He'll regret his decision.'

'Doubtful.'

While she wasn't ancient, she was a good ten years older than her ex's fiancée and her complete opposite in every way. Kara was not a fashionista, nor did she need a man to complete her. She didn't mind working hard for all she had and never planned to be a kept woman.

'I was like him once. Years ago.' His rough sandpaper textured voice drew her attention and she turned toward him. 'All that mattered to me was money, fame and fortune. I didn't understand the things in life with true worth. I made senior partner, married a beautiful woman and obtained everything I wanted. The problem came when I had to maintain them, spending eighty hours a week working until that was all I had left.'

She'd heard a little about the youngest partner. With a staff less than twenty there was bound to be chatter. Even a senior partner wasn't safe from gossip. From what she could remember he'd only been married briefly. His wife had met a tragic end. She wasn't certain of the circumstances but it was said she'd been lonely, a needy woman who demanded attention and had sought solace in pills until one day she hadn't woken up. Brendan had been beside himself. It was rumoured that the partners had been worried about his mental health until all of sudden he'd come good. Even to this day no one knew why or how.

'Then one day at a regular staff meeting in you walked. Your first week on the job. You smiled and said good morning and everything seemed to be so much brighter. All because of that smile.'

He touched the sunstone ring she'd slipped on her finger. 'I wanted to give back some of the joy you gave me.'

Kara blinked at him. She'd been responsible for his turnabout? She hadn't known. He'd never appeared to have noticed her before but, from what he'd said, for years she'd been in his thoughts.

What was she to make of that?

He stepped away awkwardly as though he'd revealed too much. 'I should leave.'

'What? Why? You're going to miss the show.'

Already the noise level had grown out on the boats and on the streets until it encompassed them like a thick blanket and she had to strain to hear him.

'I'm not sure I can start another year without you in my arms, Kara and being so close, temptation may just get the better of me.'

He smiled when she widened her eyes. 'If you haven't guessed it already, I'm in love with you.'

Her mouth opened and shut several times before she was able to speak. 'I don't know what to say.'

'Say you'll give us a chance. I know you, Kara. You're a warm, kind woman. I'm smart enough to see the gem that is you and want to hold on as tightly as I can.'

~ * ~

Something like suspicion filled her almond-shaped baby blues. Brendan hated that she questioned his motives. Though he could hardly blame her. Just a few feet away from where they stood, her ex was receiving congratulatory handshakes.

'I'm a patient man, Kara. I can wait.'

Hadn't he been waiting? For years he'd been in love with her. Her kindness shined through. She'd been treated poorly by Parker. If it had been up to Brendan, he would've kicked Parker out the door but instead the man had been promoted to junior partner. All because of the support Kara had given him. She had made him seem exceptional. With her no longer at his back his flaws were much more noticeable, the most damning, his throwing the multi-talented Kara away for a piece of fluff who was more into what she could get for herself.

A real partnership was beneficial for both parties, hadn't he learned that the hard way? He'd been blinded by beauty, believing the outside more important on his arm than a woman with her own mind, confident in her abilities.

Not that his wife had been useless. She'd been exactly what he'd wanted. He'd been the one to fail, ignoring her and her increasing neediness. Her death would forever bear a mark on his soul—and his heart. He had loved her. In a shallow, self-serving way. Now he was older. He'd learned from his past mistakes.

Kara gazed at him, the top of her head level with his shoulders. 'What do you know about me?'

'You're the first to offer to help someone in need, often sacrificing your personal time to do so. You're the one who remembers birthdays and arranges cakes. Not so long ago you were quick to joke and when you smile, a dimple appears in your left cheek.'

Kara's breath halted. He'd startled her with his observations. Coming on strong wasn't what he wanted. He'd told her he would wait. And he would. He wanted her comfortable with him, not concerned she'd attracted the attention of a stalker.

'This is crazy,' she muttered and he had a sense she was speaking to herself.

Wrapping her arms around her voluptuous body, she stared back at him, her brow furrowed as if he was some sort of complicated equation she couldn't work out.

'Why?'

Now he was confused. 'Why what?'

'Why me?'

'Is that so hard to believe? I know you've been treated poorly but you're an amazing woman. The happiest day I had in years was learning you were no longer seeing Parker.'

'It was?'

He moved closer, taking her in his arms. She tilted her head back to look up at him, displaying the slender column of her neck. Brendan held himself in check, fighting the urge to lean down and nibble.

'Yes.'

'You never said anything.'

'Of course not. I wasn't about to ruin your happiness. So I kept my feelings to myself. Until now. I didn't think I'd have a chance to tell you, and then you came bursting out here, interrupting my solace. It seemed like a sign.'

His hands settled on her waist, the soft fabric of her dress scrunching beneath his fingers as they tightened, feeling the heat of her skin.

She may not remember that day but he did, drowning in self-pity and alcohol. He'd been on a downward spiral with no desire to return. Then Kara had walked in, all sunshine and smiles.

He'd known since that first meeting that she was something special and every day since then had only fortified that feeling.

Walking out of the conference room, he'd felt invigorated for the first time in months, determined to change, to be the man she deserved. By the time he got himself organised it had been too late. Parker had wormed his way into her embrace; a patient man, he waited knowing one day he would have his chance. Now here they were and he was terrified of making a mistake.

Surprise flittered across her beautiful face as she took in how expertly he'd manoeuvred her against him, though she made no move to step away. His heart raced. Could she be considering he wasn't such a bad catch after all? Should he dare to hope?

A moment later he had his answer as Kara placed her palms on his chest, searing his skin as she slid them up to steal around his neck, her fingers playing with the hair at the nape. He shivered.

'You've waited for me all this time?'

He let out a relieved breath. There was no suspicion in her soft voice, just wonder.

'You're worth waiting for.'

Kara smiled, the dimple flashing in her left cheek. His heart raced. What that smile did to him!

'I feel as though I'm dreaming.'

'Then we both are, and if that's the case then I don't want to wake up. Not now that you're here with me.'

She swallowed hard, her body lightly trembling. Was he scaring her? Should he pull back? Go slower? He'd never been good at this whole thing. Give him a courtroom any day. Matters of the heart were different. Kara was too important.

Her eyes sparkled with unshed tears prettier than the fairy lights nearby. Her arms tightened around his neck. 'You keep saying just the right thing.'

'I've had a lot of time to prepare. Years of imagined conversations asking you if you'd like to have dinner with me. Would you?'

An eyebrow rose in amusement. 'And sneaky too.'

His fingers caressed her through the thin red fabric of her dress. She looked utterly breathtaking, though in his opinion there wasn't a day she didn't. 'I try.'

He waited silently while inside he was a mess. Only Kara seemed to have this effect on him. Whether he made progress or not, he would still count tonight as a win, standing close to her, holding her. If not tonight, one day he would erase Parker from her memories, heal the hurt inside her, build that confidence and joy that had drawn him to her and pulled him from his own pain.

'I would very much like to spend the New Year getting to know you.'

His bones melted as he relaxed, which only brought him closer to Kara. A fact he didn't mind at all. The scent of apples and vanilla tickled his nostrils. Her shampoo? Her perfume? The possibilities were endless. And he wanted to find out.

Leaning down, he covered her soft lips with his, keeping the pressure feather light ... a promise. Kara had other ideas, pulling him closer as he began to break away, deepening the kiss. Her taste burst in his mouth, a mixture of grapes and mint.

Explosions erupted around him and a round of cheers reached his ears before fading away until it seemed he and Kara were the only ones in the world. The feel of her in his arms would stay with him for the rest of his life, just as that first day would. She'd changed his life.

He caught her hand as she dropped her arms from around his neck and rested her palm over his wildly beating heart; the sunstone, moored in her ring, reflected the bright array of fireworks above their heads. He didn't bother looking up, the most beautiful vision was right in front of him.

'Happy New Year, Kara. May this year bring you great joy.'

She smiled. A butterfly danced in his stomach like a trapped bird. 'It already has.'

Staring into her eyes, Brendan saw what wasn't there before. Hope. Happiness. Trust. A future. He supposed, in their own way they'd each given the gift of healing.

For the Love of a Pug

By

Cat Whelan

'Get your humping dog away from my baby. This isn't a doggy brothel you know.' *I can't believe it! He just laughed at me.*

'Sorry, he's a little excited. He's been cooped up in this cooler weather.'

Finally he drags his enormous mutt away.

About time. Poor Ava. She looks positively frightened.

'Oh baby girl. Did that bad doggy get too friendly?'

'Err, lady I hate to tell you, but it looks like someone else got friendly with her before Felix did.' I look up from my sprawled position on the wet grass as he starts laughing. Felix clearly isn't happy about being detained from chatting up the pretty female. He is running around his owner, wrapping the lead tightly around long jean-clad legs. The tall fellow wobbles in circles as he attempts to unravel himself from the trap, his sneakered foot sliding on the slippery ground. Felix is a strong, stubborn bull-mastiff and is determined to sniff the new girl's butt.

Is it wrong to watch with amusement as Felix drags his owner to the soggy ground? I can't contain my laughter any longer and stand up to observe the show between giant dog and now grass-stained wet master. Even Ava, sitting sedately, appears to be grinning. Okay so she *is* a pug, and they permanently wear that comical smile, but I'm *sure* she took some pleasure in the antics of the two battling males as well.

'Looks like Felix rules the roost. You need a small dog like a pug.' The cute fellow starts laughing now too.

Damn, that just made him even cuter. And his dog is actually adorable. How can I stay mad at a guy with a gorgeous dog?

Trying to pick himself up while Felix continues to tug on his lead is a challenge. Poor man.

'Funny you should mention that. I'm dog-sitting Felix for my brother, but my son has been nagging me to get a pug ever since he watched a re-run of *Men In Black*. Want to trade mine for yours?' He nods his curly head to my gorgeous Ava with a chuckle.

'I would never part with her, but as you tactlessly pointed out, she had a litter six weeks ago. I'm a registered breeder.' I rummage around in my leopard print handbag for a business card.

'Sunstone Pugs,' he read aloud. 'Maggie Blackson, Registered Breeder'. Pocketing the card he pats Felix's head with a reassuring murmur. Felix who seems to have finally realised that he isn't going to get as close to the four-legged lady as he wishes, sits down at the man's feet and begins chewing on a shoelace.

'Coincidence or fate I wonder? Jacob will kill me if I don't follow through on this.' He sighs to himself, almost in resignation.

'How many puppies do you have left in the litter, and when can I see them? I really *was* serious about my son wanting one.' I bent down to rub Ava's ears in the way that always calms her down. I didn't want her worried about homes for her babies. My daughter tells me I over-react, but a mother is a mother, human or canine, right?

'I only have two not already sold. But how do you even know a pug will suit your family? And I don't know anything about you and do *not* let our precious babies go to just anybody.'

Okay that sounded a bit snotty, but really, did this man honestly think I would just hand a puppy over for him to pop under his arm and take home like a bag of fish and chips?

He smiles, and my train of protests halt. *Damn, he is sexy.*

Felix is getting restless again, pulling at his leash. Reaching into his pocket, the man draws out a small card and hands it to me.

'That's me. I'm an honest guy, would love a pug for my seven year old son and have done my research. I know they're a friendly family breed and love to be with you ALL the time.' I chuckle hearing this. He *has* done some research it seems.

'I also found out they don't like the heat, and you need to watch how much you feed them because they are food monsters, and have a tendency to get too chubby. How am I going?' He looks at me with large grey eyes.

What was the question again? Oh yes.

'You have done well Mr   ' I look at the card in my hands. 'Stapleton.'

My brain went blank.

Oh. My. God. Mitchell Stapleton. This man is the CEO of the multi-million dollar advertising firm I used to work for. Until I quit and became a pug breeder.

At least I know he can *afford* a puppy. He could afford to buy my property several hundred times over.

'Right, well I have to head off as the puppies are due for their dinner. Give me a call if you really are interested, and we'll arrange a viewing.' I tug gently on Ava's lead to signal our departure. She gives Felix a disdainful look and stands up.

'I'll call you. Talk about a coincidental meeting. I'll have to thank my brother for letting me dog-sit after all. Come on Felix.' He turns to head towards the park gate and disappears into the surrounding trees as though I have imagined the whole event. Ava, anxious to get back to her puppies, tugs me towards the car. Jumping into my white Camry, she as usual, has to be coaxed out of the driver's seat. *Cheeky girl.*

'Well, that was interesting. I wonder if we'll hear from him again.' Ava grins back at me, probably just hoping she is going to receive a treat when we get home.

~ * ~

There is a phone demanding an answer somewhere, reminding me why I have left a stressful life, moved to country South Australia, and now breed loving, friendly, low maintenance pugs. Their perpetual smiles and amusing clown-like personalities never fail to make me smile, and remind me not to take life too seriously. On the verge of a work overload, and in the middle of a divorce, I realised my life needed to change before I had a blowout. I took my two kids, bought a large property, and moved fifty kilometres away. We never looked back. That was three years ago.

Placing the black pug puppy I was cuddling back in the pen with its siblings, I rush to find the annoying phone. A necessary evil in my business.

'Hello, Sunstone Pugs, Maggie speaking.'

'Hi Maggie.' *Mm-sexy voice from the dog park. He didn't waste any time. Must be serious about a puppy.*

'I met you yesterday, at the park. Large frisky dog. My companion, not me.' That deep chuckle sent a tingle through my torso.

'I remember Felix very well Mr Stapleton. Ava's still traumatised.' I laugh along with him.

'I'm calling to see when I could swing by and see your puppies. I really *am* keen to get one for my son. He visits me every other week and is apparently *dying* for a pug friend.'

'Ah well we can't have any kids dying from lack of a pug. I'm free either today or tomorrow afternoon. There are only two pups left and I have another viewing this afternoon at four o'clock.'

'I'll be there at two o'clock then. That way I can choose which one I want.'

'I'll see you at two then. The address is on the card. 'Bye Mr Stapleton.'

'It's Mitchell. And I think I may call you Maggie seeing you used to work for me. See you later.'

He hung up before my shock wore off.

~ * ~

As I lift the puppy he points to out of the pen, and hand it to him, our eyes meet as fingers lightly brush in the puppy transfer.

Did he feel that jolt too? Maggie you're acting like a desperate old maid. Get a hold of yourself. He just wants a puppy.

Watching Mitchell gently cradling the tiny puppy in his large hands, cooing quietly in its velvety ears, I realise he has an effect on canine females as well as human ones. The puppy was snuffling contentedly into his palm, enjoying the warm contact.

'So tell me, why does a successful advertising executive quit her job and move to the country to breed dogs?' Bam, straight to the point.

'I Googled you when I realised your name was familiar.' He looks sheepishly at me, still caressing the little puglet softly.

Lucky puppy.

You need a cold shower, Maggie. And maybe an online purchase from an adult's store. The kind that arrives in discreet packaging.

I stand in front of him, arms folded, chin tilted proudly.

'I woke up one day and found my daughter sitting on my bed sobbing. She had the lead in her school musical and her father had informed her he couldn't go. She already suspected my dedication to my job would keep me from getting there too. It was then I realised she assumed I would let her down, and that she was used to coming second to my career. I was gutted. That day I called in sick, and we sat together and made a new family plan. I handed in my resignation the following day, and we went house shopping. Followed by dog shopping.' I wave my arms around to indicate the little world I have built for us.

'Tough call. Has it been worth it?'

'Every single day. I wake up energised instead of struggling to breathe and battling to get through each day. The kids are happy here and help me with the dogs. It's the best move we ever made.'

'Sunstone Pugs, where does that name come from?' The puppy has managed to crawl up and snuggle into his neck by now, snoring softly. He looks at it with adoration already.

Oh dear. This is where he'll think I am kooky. May as well get it over with.

'When I was having a hard time with my divorce, a friend gave me this crystal pendant. It's a sunstone. It apparently rebalances one's emotional patterns, optimism, and enthusiasm and encourages self-empowerment and independence. It encourages the willingness and ability to bestow blessings on others.' I shrug self-consciously as I hold the gold-coloured stone that means so much to me.

'I decided that's all of the things we were going to try to do and be in our new lives. And we decided to bestow blessings in the form of pug puppies. Who doesn't love a pug?' I attempt a laugh to lighten the mood.

'Their little squishy faces remind me of a teddy bear. They are eternally happy.' I can't gauge the look he is throwing me from those sexy grey eyes. I turn away and pretend I'm busy with the puppy pen. I haven't heard him wander over to stand next to me, watching the puppies playing, tumbling, pouncing and biting each other. His voice close and soft, startles me.

'Well, I'm blessed you have puggies. And I think this little lady would like to come home with me when she is ready.'

What female wouldn't?

Wait! Stop that Maggie. You're not his type. You could have been, but you left that world.

'Well she's a little cutie that one, even though she *is* the runt. She's feisty and keeps all the others in line.' I can't resist ruffling her soft ears.

'I *like* feisty females.' He chuckles and I realise he is staring at me intently.

Is he still talking about the dog? And why is he looking at me as though I am a puppy?

He leans down to place the now wiggling baby back with her siblings.

Damn he has a cute butt. Double damn, he just caught me checking it out! A sexy smile makes his eyes sparkle cheekily. My face flushes with embarrassment and he laughs. Which makes me cringe even more. Clearly he thinks I am like all the women he probably meets. Desperate to get his attention, and devour his delectable body.

Not this woman. I don't need anybody.

Squaring my shoulders and lifting my chin, I make sure he knows this was about business only.

'The puppy can be picked up in two more weeks Mr Stapleton. I'll email the payment details and see you in a fortnight.' Realising this was his cue to leave, Mitchell nods. I ignore the questioning look on his face at my abrupt dismissal. Just as I try to ignore his solid, masculine form as he saunters back down my driveway.

Damn.

~ * ~

It's puppy pick-up day. There's only one little bundle left chewing the blanket as she plays, oblivious to how her world is about to change. I wait too with butterflies taking flight in my belly as I hear a car pull up in the driveway.

You were okay when the other puppies were picked up. What's wrong with you?

'Hi Maggie.' I spin around with carefully placed surprise on my face.

'Oh, hi Mr Stapleton. I didn't hear you arrive.' *Liar.* I reach into the pen and pick up the remaining bundle of love and turn to her new owner. *What the? He was checking out my butt. Payback I suppose.*

'Your girl is ready to go to her new home. Does your son know about her yet?' I reluctantly hand her over to him, ignoring the spark that jumps from my hand to his. *Static electricity from his car, no doubt.*

'No, it's going to be a surprise. He's been pretty down in the dumps since his Mum and I divorced, and I want to give him something to look forward to when he visits. I can't wait to see his face.' His grin just about split his face in two. He really *was* excited about his new baby. At least I know she'll be well loved. Another blessing bestowed by Sunstone Pugs.

'I'm sure he'll never want to leave once he meets this little darling. I'll miss her terribly. She usually follows me around everywhere when they're out of the pen and has really wormed her way into my heart.' Stroking her back gently, I feel warmth well in my chest, up through my throat and onto my face. The emotion took hold quickly. *Damn it. I can't cry in front of him.*

Dipping my head, I try to hide my watery eyes. When I feel a soft touch on my shoulder and a reassuring rub, I know I've been discovered.

'Maggie, I'll take good care of her, I promise. And you can come and visit, or we'll come back and visit you and Ava.'

I keep my head down trying to compose myself. *What the hell was going on? Was it because I felt a strong bond with this puppy? Maybe I was hormonal? Maybe it was a full moon?*

A rough hand gently lifts my chin so I have to look him in the face. Those grey eyes are tender, and his expression not unlike the adoring one he has towards the puppy.

'If you let me, I'd like to spend more time with you anyway.' My heart skids, then takes off again at a gallop.

Surely I misheard that. The CEO of a multi-million dollar company wanted to spend time with a little pug breeder? The shock must be written all over my face, and my voice has forgotten its job. I am frozen.

'Of course if you think it is unprofessional to have anything to do with your dog owners, I understand.' He averts his eyes and drops that comforting hand from my shoulder.

Put it back! I haven't felt like this in a very long time. Wake up Maggie!

'Err, okay that sounds good.' *Oh brilliant Mags, he'll think you're dumb as a doorpost.*

He smiles down at me again, light shining in his wolf-like eyes. His eyebrows lift.

'Really? That's great. I want to get to know you better and find out what makes you tick. You're a rare woman Maggie. From what little I already know, I have found you to be courageous, straight forward, intelligent, caring. You go after what you want. I like that about you.' My insides quivered.

He likes something about me. Wow. Maybe I misjudged him after all.

'From what I've been told through my company, you were an asset to us. But from what I see you're producing here,' he held up the squirming puppy, '*this* is more precious than making more money or buying more advertising air-time. You're promoting love, family bonds, and lasting friendships. A dog brings together a home. Grounds it in fun and fur.' He gently reaches out and places his free hand over mine, warm and rough. '*That* is priceless.'

Oh my God. He gets it. I feel warmth spread throughout my body, almost in relief. I'm used to being judged in my decision to leave a corporate well-paid job, uproot my children, and move to the country.

I place my hand on top of his larger one and smile widely.

'Thank you. And Ava and I can't wait to spend time with you and your puppy.'

'Her name is Sunny.' We both laugh as Sunny's rough tongue licks our hands in approval.

Little Gems

2017

Onyx

Black, or black banded with white, also red or brown

A hard stone

Popular with ancient Greeks and Romans